THE WORLD'S WORST CHILDREN 2

Books by David Walliams:

THE BOY IN THE DRESS
MR STINK
BILLIONAIRE BOY
GANGSTA GRANNY
RATBURGER
DEMON DENTIST
AWFUL AUNTIE
GRANDPA'S GREAT ESCAPE
THE MIDNIGHT GANG
BAD DAD
THE ICE MONSTER
THE BEAST OF BUCKINGHAM PALACE
CODE NAME BANANAS
GANGSTA GRANNY STRIKES AGAIN!
SPACEBOY

FING
SLIME
MEGAMONSTER
ROBODOG

THE WORLD'S WORST CHILDREN 1
THE WORLD'S WORST CHILDREN 2
THE WORLD'S WORST CHILDREN 3
THE WORLD'S WORST TEACHERS
THE WORLD'S WORST PARENTS
THE WORLD'S WORST PETS

Also available in picture book:

THE SLIGHTLY ANNOYING ELEPHANT
THE FIRST HIPPO ON THE MOON
THE QUEEN'S ORANG-UTAN
THE BEAR WHO WENT BOO!
THERE'S A SNAKE IN MY SCHOOL!
BOOGIE BEAR
GERONIMO
LITTLE MONSTERS
MARMALADE
GRANNYSAURUS

David Walliams

THE WORLD'S WORST CHILDREN 2

ILLUSTRATED BY *Tony Ross*

HarperCollins *Children's Books*

DAVID WALLIAMS

For
all my friends at
Northern Counties
School, with love
D.W.

TONY ROSS

For
Kate, Lucy D, and
the Kerswell Gang,
the real Macoys
T.R.

First published in the United Kingdom by
HarperCollins *Children's Books* in 2017
First published in this revised paperback edition in 2023
HarperCollins *Children's Books* is a division of
HarperCollins*Publishers* Ltd,
1 London Bridge Street, London SE1 9GF
www.harpercollins.co.uk
HarperCollins*Publishers*,
Macken House, 39/40 Mayor Street Upper,
Dublin 1, D01 C9W8, Ireland
1

Find out more about HarperCollins and the
environment at
www.harpercollins.co.uk/green

THANK-YOUS

I would like to thank some of the world's worst grown-ups who helped me with the book.

First of all my *illustrator*, **TONY ROSS**, who goes into bookshops and defaces other illustrators' work by drawing incredibly rude things on top.

Then there is *Executive Publisher*, **ANN-JANINE MURTAGH**. She drags authors through stinging nettles if they don't hand in their books on time.

All hail the *CEO* of HarperCollins, **CHARLIE REDMAYNE**, who demands that everyone in the office calls him "His Royal Highness King Charlie".

My *literary agent*, **PAUL STEVENS**, must be thanked. He covers up the fact that he is completely bald by strapping a live hamster to his head.

There's my *editor*, **ALICE BLACKER**, who likes to break wind violently and then blame it on the nice lady at the next desk.

The *Publishing Director*, **KATE BURNS**, does a fine job of sneezing on people's puddings on purpose so she can finish them off herself.

The *Managing Editor*, **SAMANTHA STEWART**, is better known as the phantom pen thief. She has a collection of 20,000 stolen pens.

Across from her sits the *Creative Director*, **VAL BRATHWAITE**, who spends all day eating her own belly-button fluff.

The *Art Director*, **DAVID McDOUGALL**, who refuses to work unless he has a pair of underpants on his head.

My *cover designer*, **KATE CLARKE**, who likes to play tricks on people. Kate staples ladies' dresses to their chairs so they rip when they stand up, leaving the bottom area exposed for all the world to see.

My *text designer*, **ELORINE GRANT**, seems nice enough, but inside that giant jar of "gobstoppers" she has on her desk to share are really glass eyes.

The *PR Director*, **GERALDINE STROUD**... She is the worst. Geraldine threatens to duff up children in bookshops if they don't buy my books. I am actually all for this.

My *publicist*, **SAM WHITE**, should not be thanked as she never does a scrap of work. Instead she passes the time prising out the smelliest, yellowest earwax and flicking it at people.

And finally a thank-you to my *audio editor*, **TANYA HOUGHAM**. A thoroughly cruel character, she sticks superglue to your headphones, so after recording an audiobook they are stuck to your head forever.

David Walliams

From the desk of
H.R.H. THE QUEEN

Dear reader,

It is with enormous personal pleasure and
pride that one declares this book open.

This is a great moment not just for
Great Britain and the Commonwealth
nations, but for all the people of the world.

One is a **huge** admirer of the author David Walliams. In fact, it seems most peculiar I haven't awarded him an honour yet. *Dame David Walliams*. That is much better.

One is a huge admirer of Dame David Walliams, and this **magnificent book**, *The World's Worst Children 2*, which one is told is a sequel to *The World's Worst Children* (who knew?), and which is sure to be regarded as one of the greatest works of literature of all time.

One is not at all miffed that once again that irritating squirt Walliams has put me in his book as a character and not paid me a penny.

Yours royally,

Her Majesty the Queen

CONTENTS

Gruesome
GRISELDA p.165

Spoiled
BRAD p.187

TRISH
the Troll p.209

Competitive
COLIN p.233

No No
NOE p.257

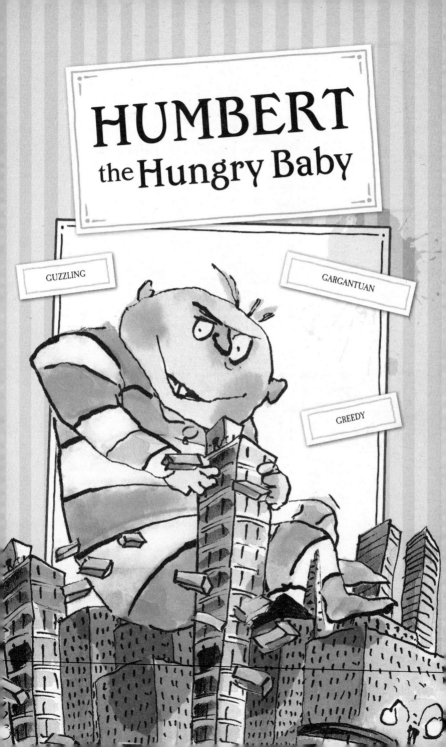

HUMBERT
the Hungry Baby

"OH MY!" EXCLAIMED the midwife when she delivered the baby. It was the biggest tot the lady had ever seen in her many years of delivering them.
He plopped on to the floor of the hospital like a beached whale.

"Oh my word!" cried the father.

How had this skinny bean of a man helped create such a ginormous baby?

"Is he beautiful?" asked the baby's anxious mother. She couldn't see her newborn child from where she was lying on the bed.

"Well, you know they say 'big is beautiful'," replied the father.

"Yes?"

"He is definitely big."

"How big exactly?"

"Just let me weigh him for you, missus!" called out the midwife. With great effort, she hauled this monster baby on to the scales, which immediately broke under his weight.

TWANG!

"How much does my darling boy weigh?" asked Mother.

The midwife studied the boy. "I would say no more than a baby hippopotamus."

"I need to see him!" pleaded Mother.

The midwife had to enlist the boy's father to heave the infant up on to his mother's chest.

"OOF!" The poor woman was squashed. Her face went bright purple and her eyes bulged. It looked as if they might pop out of her head.

"I CAN'T BREATHE!"

she mouthed.

When the pair had managed to heave the enormous lump off his mother, Father asked, "Darling, whatever shall we call him?"

"Humbert!" she said. "Little Humbert!"

"*Little* Humbert?" asked Father, a hint of sarcasm in his voice.

The new parents had brought a pretty pram to the hospital, in which to take their baby home. However, as soon as Humbert was lowered into it, the pram was flattened.

CRUNCH!!

The pair hijacked a forklift truck so they could get their offspring home. They just managed to squeeze him through the front door. On seeing the size of him, Marmalade the family cat dashed through the cat flap.

Somehow the parents hauled him up the stairs. As soon as they had lowered him into his cot, he burst out of it.

BOOM!

Shards of wood exploded across his nursery, smashing everything in sight. The room looked as if a bomb had hit it.

"Where's he going to sleep now?" asked Father.

"In our bed, of course!" replied Mother.

So their bedroom became Humbert's nursery, and the baby **sprawled** out on their double bed.

Mother slept on the sofa downstairs and

Father had to sleep
standing
up
in
a
cupboard.

Not that the pair got any sleep.

If they stopped feeding their new baby milk for more than a minute, Humbert would scream the house down.

Such was the noise that the walls would shake, the roof would rattle and the windows would crack.

One bottle of milk was never enough. As soon as Humbert had his lips round the first bottle, the second would have to be filled. Then the next. And the next. And the next. The baby would only stop to do one thing. Burp.

"*BURP!!!*"

Guzzling all that milk down, Humbert began expanding at an alarming rate.

When there was no milk left in the house, Humbert would wail for food again.

"WHAAA!!!"

If he wasn't immediately brought something to eat, he would roll out of bed...

THUD!

and he would lollop down... the stairs...

like a giant slug...

trying to breakdance.

One night he demolished the entire contents of the fridge in seconds:

a WHOLE trifle

a huge block of **cheese**

a foot-long salami sausage

egg

after egg

after egg

and a pack of butter, including the wrapping in which it came.

In the morning, Humbert had his innocent face on.
However, his **burp** gave him away.

"**BURP!!!**"

It was a cheesy eggy buttery meaty trifley burp that
blew straight into his parents' faces like a hurricane.

Upon seeing the carnage in the kitchen, Father was
furious. "I don't believe it! There's not a thing
left in here to eat!"

"Well, little Humbert is a growing boy!" replied Mother.

"Growing? If he carries on like this, he'll be the size of an elephant by Christmas!" snapped Father. "I am putting a padlock on the fridge!"

"But what if little Humbert gets peckish during the night?"

"Peckish?!" exclaimed Father. "Our son is eating us out of house and home. I am going to move all the food we've got left out of his reach!"

As Mother fumed, Father did just that. He moved everything in the larder to the top shelf, which he could barely reach himself. There was no way Humbert could get his hands on the biscuits, cereals and cakes. Or so his father thought.

It wasn't long before Humbert was wailing to be fed again.

"WHAAA!"

That evening Mother gave her baby even more milk than usual. Pint after pint after pint. The woman cut the bottom off the bottle so more milk could be poured in without interrupting Humbert's feed.

"Hurry!" ordered Mother.

"I'm trying!" snapped back Father as he ran to fetch yet another carton.

When the man stumbled, running up the stairs, and dropped a carton, it burst on to the floor.

"WHAAA!" Humbert wailed.

Then he simply ate the bottle.

"My goodness, he *must* be full now!" remarked Father.

CRUNCH!

"BURP!"

"Night-night, little Humbert," said Mother, planting a kiss on her baby's forehead.

Humbert did a big wet milky burp right in his mother's face.

"BURP!!!"

Father smirked.

"Come on, darling, it's been another exhausting day," said the man. "Let's try to get some sleep."

Mother lay on the sofa, and Father shut himself in the cupboard. They both fell asleep.

"ZZZZ... ZZZZ..."

"ZZZZ... ZZZZ..."

Moments later Humbert wailed.

"WHAAA!!!"

As his parents were asleep, no one came running, so the big baby **rolled** himself out of bed.

THUD!

He poured himself down the stairs and slithered into the kitchen. As the food had all been placed out of reach, the baby had to find a way to grab it.

First he tried bouncing. Humbert was perfectly round, but he was just too heavy to become airborne. Next he reached for a cooking pot to stand on, but he still couldn't reach any food. So the baby pulled over a thick cookbook, and placed that on top of the pot. Still he couldn't reach the food. So he dragged poor Marmalade over by her tail.

"MIAOW!"

screeched the cat.

Humbert placed the cat on top of the pile. He stepped on her with his big fleshy foot. "MIAOW!"

Humbert's eyes widened as he finally saw what he'd been looking for.

Food. Glorious food.

The big baby was still standing on top of the cat. As his feet pressed down on the poor creature, she let out a series of loud yelps. It was as if he was playing the bagpipes.

"*MIAoooow! MIAOW!*"

Before long, Humbert had grabbed every can, box and packet of food.

Then he began his fantastic feast.

First, Humbert ate his own body weight in marshmallows.

That is a lot of marshmallows.

"BURP!!!"

Then he gobbled down a
variety pack of cereals.
Boxes and all.

Next the big baby set
to work on the tinned
puddings. Rice pudding.

Pineapple chunks.

Chocolate sponge.

Being a baby, Humbert didn't know how to
use a tin opener. So he ate the tins too.

Next the baby found a large jar of mustard. It smelled funny. Humbert poked his fingers in and grabbed a mouthful. "EURGH!"

Like most children, Humbert didn't like the taste of mustard at all. He spat it out of his mouth...

"PFFT!"

...and hurled the jar across the kitchen. A streak of mustard was splashed on to the floor.

HUMBERT THE HUNGRY BABY

Humbert desperately needed to eat something to take the taste away.

The big baby jumped down and looked around the kitchen.

There was not a scrap of food left to eat. He had scoffed the lot. The larder was empty. The fridge was empty.

Humbert licked the wall to take the hot mustard off his tongue, but still it tasted off.

Poor Marmalade hadn't liked being trodden on one bit, and was now curled up in her basket.

Humbert looked at Marmalade.

Marmalade looked back at Humbert.

Could he?

Should he?

Would he?

"*MIAOW!*"

Yes. He would.

The poor cat was gobbled down in one gulp.

The next morning, Mother and Father went to the kitchen to make breakfast. As he strode in, in his pyjamas, Father slipped on the mustard.

"OW!"

He shot across the kitchen floor and ended up covered in the stuff.

wHoOsH!

"Oh, you silly man!" exclaimed Mother.

"I didn't leave it there!" he protested, vainly trying to rub the mustard off his pyjamas. "In fact, I put this with everything else on the top shelf, out of reach of you-know-who!"

Suspicious, Father opened the door of the larder. "Once again there's not a thing left to eat in the house! We are going to starve!"

The man dashed upstairs to the bedroom, and as usual Humbert was sprawled out on what used to be his parents' double bed. After his latest midnight feast, he had expanded during the night, and was now getting too big for the room.

"BBBUUuRRRPPP!!!"

went the baby.

It was so loud the house shook.

RATTLE!

Out of the baby's mouth came a giant orange fur ball.

"**I DON'T BELIEVE IT!**" shouted Father.
"**HE'S EATEN THE CAT!**"

Mother rushed upstairs and burst into the room.
"No!"
"Look!" said Father, indicating the fur ball.

"Well, silly old Marmalade must have wandered into poor little Humbert's mouth during the night,"
mused Mother.

"She wasn't a fly!
Marmalade was a cat.
A big furry cat!"

"BBBB*BUUUURRPP*"!!!!!!!

It was a burp that could make an ancient city crumble to the ground.

Mother and Father had to cling on to each other to make sure they didn't fall over.

"The naughty cat has given my poor little Humbert indigestion! Quickly, Father, call an ambulance!"

Father did what he was told. He rushed out of the bedroom to the downstairs telephone.

"Hello? I need an ambulance, please. It's my baby son. He's just eaten a cat. No, the cat wasn't cooked – it was raw..."

"AAAAAAAAAH!"

came a cry from upstairs.

This was followed by a thunderous...

"BBBBBBUUUU UURRRR RRRRPPPPP!"

"...and I think he may have just eaten my wife! Yes, raw. Please come as fast as you can!"

Father slammed the telephone down and dashed up the stairs.

Opening the bedroom door, he saw that his wife's feet were just poking out of his baby son's mouth. Humbert munched on his mother's pink fluffy slippers.

"BURP!"

Right in front of Father's eyes, Humbert was getting bigger and bigger and bigger. It was as if the baby was a lilo being inflated.

The bed collapsed under his weight.

CRUNCH!

Unsteadily, Humbert rose to his feet. The baby was now taller than Father and his head hit the ceiling.

A blizzard of plaster filled the room.

THUD!

Through the cloud Father could make out his baby son advancing towards him, gobbling up everything in sight.

A shelf of books.
"BURP!"

An armchair.
"BURP!"

The dressing table.
"BURP!"

Panic flashed across Father's face. In that moment he realised something. Something terrible...

He was next!

NEE-NAW! NEE-NAW!

The ambulance was near.

Father had to get out of the house. And fast.

He slid down the banister...

wHOOSH!

...and reached the front door. Frantically, he started unlocking it.

Looking back, he glimpsed Humbert hurtling down the stairs on his giant bottom, sending pictures on the wall flying.

SMASH! BANG! WALLOP!

If Humbert didn't eat his father, he was sure to flatten him.

Still in his mustard-soaked pyjamas, the man dashed out of the front door, slamming it behind him.

That didn't stop Humbert.

Oh no.

The baby smashed through the front wall of the house…

KABOOM!

…sending bricks tumbling through the air. They fell to the ground all around Father.

THUD!

THUD! THUD!

With the front wall gone, the whole house began to crumble…

CRACK!

…and collapsed to the ground in an explosion of dust and debris.

Father ran and hid behind a bush.

NEE-NAW! NEE-NAW!

The ambulance screeched to a halt outside what was left of the family home.

As soon as it had stopped, Humbert lumbered over to it. He picked up the ambulance with ease.

"ARGH!" screamed the ambulance driver as he leaped out of the door, landing on the ground with a thud. "OOF!"

He looked up in horror as the giant baby crushed the ambulance with his bare hand.

CRUNCH! "wHAAA!!!"

Humbert was hungry again.

He took a humongous bite out of the ambulance.

"BURP!" And another. "BURP!"

Until he'd swallowed it down.

- 46 -

"GULP! BURP!"

Father was still hiding behind the bush, but decided it would be safer to make a run for it. He raced down the street, but the giant baby **thundered** after him.

BOOM!
BOOM! BOOM!

Each step was like an earthquake.

Humbert grabbed a passing poodle and ate that.

"BURP!"

The little old lady out walking the poodle didn't let go of the lead so she was gobbled up too.

Father ran and ran. Still the giant baby chased him.

A tree was upended, and munched into a pulp.

"BURP!"

Then a double-decker bus was gobbled up.

Next a squad of police cars raced down the road. They stopped in formation to create a roadblock. One by one the cars were tossed up in the air and caught in the baby's mouth like peanuts.

"BURP!"

Humbert grew bigger and bigger and bigger the more he ate. He was now the size of a *Tyrannosaurus rex*.

Father ran across the bridge to the city. There he hoped the baby could not catch him.

However, the city just meant more things for Humbert to eat.

Streetlights.

Statues.

Cars.

Lorries.

Even a fire engine was gobbled up in one gulp.

"BBBUUURRRPPP!!!"

Up ahead, Father spotted
a very tall building. It must
have been a thousand floors
high. Right at the top he
was sure to be out of reach
of his ravenously hungry
baby son. There was a
glass lift at the side of the
building. Father frantically
pressed the button for floor
1,000, and began travelling
up at speed.

In the safety of the lift,
the man breathed a sigh of
relief.

PING!

The lift jolted as it reached
the very top of the building.
The doors slid open and
Father rushed out on to the
roof. When he looked down,

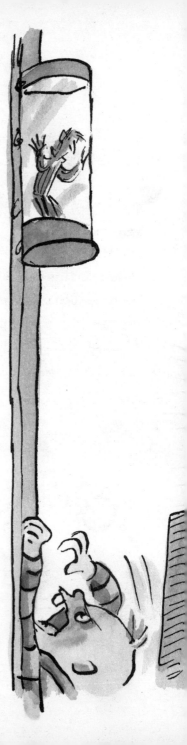

he saw that the giant baby was scaling the building.

"NOOOO!"

screamed Father.

WHIRRR!

The man turned round.

A police helicopter was buzzing overhead. The pilot leaned out with a loudhailer.

"GIANT BABY THING! PLEASE MAKE YOUR WAY DOWN TO STREET LEVEL AND STOP EATING EVERYTHING!"

Humbert reached out to grab the helicopter. He swatted it like a fly. As it began falling to the ground, the giant baby grabbed the helicopter and ate it.

"BURP!"

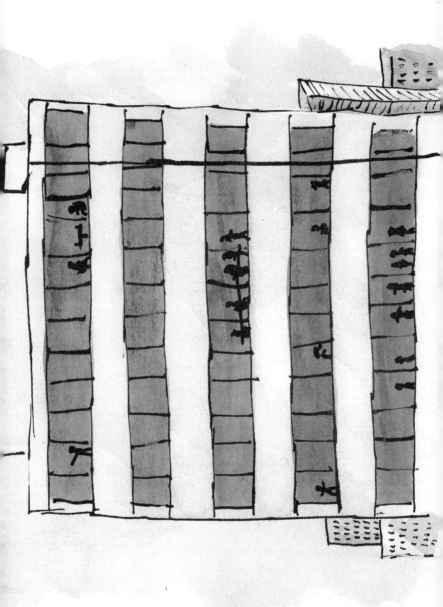

In no time, Humbert had climbed to the top of the building. Father was trapped. The baby's ginormous hand reached on to the roof and scooped up the man.

"DON'T EAT ME!" he pleaded. "I AM YOUR FATHER!"

But the baby just smiled, baring his gums.

"ARGH!" screamed the man as he disappeared into the baby's mouth.

But the baby spat him out. "YUCK!"

"THE MUSTARD!" exclaimed Father, scrambling to his feet on the roof of the building. Slipping over on the spicy sauce had saved his life.

Just then three fighter jets *whizzed* past.

"DON'T SHOOT!" shouted Father. "All we need to do is coat every man, woman and child in the world in mustard and we will all be fine!"

The baby reached out and grabbed one of the fighter jets.

He munched it down.

"BURP!"

And another.

"BURP!"

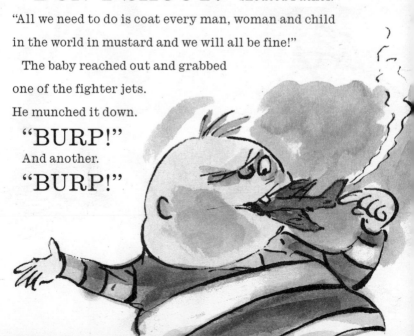

The pilot of the third jet
started to fly off at speed.
Humbert reached to grab it.
As he did, he lost his balance.

"NOOOOOOOO!"

screamed Father as the big
baby tumbled to the ground.

"WHAAA!!!"

Humbert the hungry baby was no more.

So what is the moral of this story?

It's very simple. However hungry you are, NEVER try to eat three fighter jets in one sitting. Two are more than enough.

STACEY
Superstar

STACEY
Superstar

FROM THE MOMENT she made her grand entrance into the world on the day she was born, Stacey Clog believed she was destined for stardom. By the age of ten the girl was convinced she should be the biggest star who ever lived.

In her mind she had it all **planned** out.

Stacey would reach the very top of the entertainment world, sell millions of albums and be showered with awards. Then she would play herself in a five-hour movie of her own life, entitled quite simply

Stacey Clog: The Myth Behind the Legend

In her own lifetime a huge gold statue of herself would be erected in her home town, and a museum set up in her honour. **The Clog Museum** would not house any clogs. Instead it would contain Stacey's personal collection of gowns, awards and, of course, photographs of herself wearing the gowns and holding the awards. This would ensure she would remain famous for centuries after her passing, celebrated until the end of time. And beyond.

There was just one problem.

Stacey had no talent.

When she tried to sing, the noise she made was ear-torturingly painful. It wasn't so much singing, more wailing. Despite her poor parents spending every penny they had on singing lessons for their fame-hungry daughter, Stacey never got any better. In fact, she just got worse. Every time the girl practised her singing, something terrible would happen.

Once in her Music class, at the top of her school, her teacher leaped out of the window with his hands over his ears. He never came back to the school. There are rumours he is now living in Peru under an assumed name.

When Stacey took on a huge ballad in the kitchen, her mother screamed and begged her daughter to stop. When the girl refused, and just started singing louder, the woman hid in the deep freezer. It took weeks to thaw her out.

If she practised in her bedroom, Stacey's goldfish, Beyoncé, would leap out of its bowl, and her hamster, Mariah, would leap in.

Singing in the bath one night, the tiles all exploded off the walls.

Performing Christmas carols at a school assembly, the headmistress hit the fire alarm and the school was evacuated.

Strolling in the woods and humming to herself, trees would fall behind her.

Hitting a particularly high note in a love song one night at the local community hall for a group of, thankfully deaf, old ladies, their cups smashed, showering tea all over them.

Practising scales with her Music tutor one afternoon, the lady dived into her grand piano and shut the lid tight.

Forced to rehearse at the bottom of her back garden, the shed somehow set itself alight and burned to the ground.

Standing alone on top of a hill, as soon as Stacey began singing, a flock of birds fell out of the sky and landed dead at her feet.

However, nothing could stop Stacey believing she was the world's greatest singer. She was right and everyone else was wrong. Especially her goldfish. So one day Stacey decided to enter a TV talent show. She was sure that this would be her first step to *stardom*.

The girl's mother and father begged their daughter not to audition for **The Ego Factor**. They knew it would only lead to disaster. Stacey might very well cause the judges and audience to scream for her to stop, or, even worse, laugh at her for singing so awfully.

"Are you crazy?!" protested the girl. "Stacey Clog is a winner!"

"You *are* Stacey Clog," said Mother.

"I know!" said Stacey Clog. "And I, **Stacey Clog**, will be crowned the greatest singer of all time, live on TV!"

Father tried a gentle approach. "But, my darling, what if you just have an off day..."

"**Stacey Clog** does not have an off day!" thundered Stacey Clog.

"But you *are* Stacey Clog," repeated Mother.

"I know, you fool. My audition will be a triumph. It will be forever remembered as the first step on **Stacey Clog's** journey to superstardom. No... mega-stardom! No... hyper-stardom! Just really, really, really big *stardom*. Has there ever been a time when **Stacey Clog** hasn't had an incredible reaction when she sings?"

"For the last time, you *are*—"

But before Mother could finish her sentence, Father stepped in. "No, my dearest daughter. Indeed, the reaction has been one of total incredulity."

"**Exactly!**" replied the girl. "**Stacey Clog** knows that as soon as **Stacey Clog** sings live on TV, **Stacey Clog** will become the most famous person the world has ever known."

"Oh no," murmured Father.

"...of all time."

"I thought you had finished."

"...forever and ever."

"Finished now?"

"...and ever." The girl thought for a moment. "**Yes. Stacey Clog** has finished."

The decision had been made. So forms were filled in, phone calls were made and a very expensive designer gown was bought for Stacey by selling the family car.

Finally the night of the audition came. After weeks of non-stop rehearsing, Mother had gone to live at the North Pole, so Father took his daughter to the theatre on the bus. Her dress was so huge it took up the entire back row.

As Stacey swept on to the stage, Father waited anxiously in the wings.

"What's your name?" asked the head judge, Tyson Trowel. He was a very vain man. Despite being at least ninety years old, Tyson had a strange orange spray-on tan, glow-in-the-dark teeth and a wig that sat atop his head like a crouching badger. This was the kind of man who wore sunglasses inside, in the dark. There were three other judges, but he paid them to sit there and look pretty and never speak. **The Ego Factor** was all about Tyson.

"Stacey Clog," replied the girl. "It's a name nobody will forget after tonight."

The audience all murmured to each other. Who was this girl with the huge ego?

Tyson Trowel had a short memory. "Sorry, what's your name again?"

"Stacey Clog."

"So, Stacey Clog, what are you going to sing for us today?"

"A love ballad," announced the girl. "It's about the great love of your life."

"Who will you be thinking of when you sing it?" asked Tyson.

"Me," replied Stacey.

The audience laughed. Even Tyson Trowel, who couldn't walk past a mirror without admiring himself in it, smirked.

"So, sorry, what's your name again?"

"Stacey Clog!" The girl was becoming irritated with the little man now.

"So, Stacey Clog, are you any good?"

"Humbly, Stacey Clog is the greatest singer of all time."

The audience giggled again. There had been some big-headed people auditioning on the show before, but this girl was off the scale.

"Well, sorry, what's your name again?"

"STACEY CLOG!"

"Stacey Clog. The stage is yours..."

The lights dimmed, and a spotlight picked out the girl and her huge dress, which made her look like a giant meringue.

Father had been listening backstage to his daughter, going increasingly red with embarrassment. Now it was his moment. Stacey had given her father a simple task: he was to play the backing CD for her to sing to when she nodded in his direction. However, to save his daughter from complete and utter **humiliation** live on television, the man had a secret plan. He'd swapped the backing CD with no singing on it to one with a famous singer performing the song. And just as Stacey was about to burst into song he planned to pull the plug on his daughter's microphone so nobody in the theatre or at home watching it on television could hear her. That way it would seem as if Stacey Clog had a fantastic voice, instead of one that sounded like someone dragging their nails down a blackboard.

Stacey took a deep breath, and nodded to her father. He then pressed "play" on the CD player, remembering to put in the right CD with a superstar already singing on it.

When no one backstage was looking, the man yanked the plug of her microphone out of the wall by wrapping the lead round his foot.

The music swelled.

Stacey opened her mouth to sing and the judges, the audience in the theatre, and the millions of people watching their TVs at home heard this most magical sound. Immediately the judges were all applauding and the audience was on its feet. Stacey Clog had the voice of a superstar, or so they thought.

Father put the volume of the music up as loud as it would go so it would drown out his daughter's wails.

As for Stacey, she was completely oblivious to her father's deception. This was exactly the reaction she'd been expecting from the start. Complete worship of her talent. In her mind's eye Stacey began to see her destiny. Her own private plane, **AIR CLOG ONE**.

A chauffeur-driven Rolls-Royce picking her up on the tarmac to whisk her to the stadium. A hundred white kittens to play with backstage before a show. An audience of thousands on their feet before she'd even sung a note. *The biggest diamonds* in the world dangling from her ears. Ten costume changes during each song. The stage knee-deep in flowers at the end of the concert.

Backstage, Father was smiling to himself. His plan couldn't be working any better.

However, his smile dropped as disaster struck. Just as the song reached a crescendo Stacey stamped her foot and the CD stuck.

The voice on the CD repeated a word over and over and over again.

"Love—Love— Love—Love— Love—"

The audience realised they had been fooled. Suddenly they were very, **very** angry. The girl was a cheat! The boos became deafening.

"BOO!"

In a panic Father pressed "stop" on the CD player, and rushed on to the stage to whisk his daughter off and save her from the angry mob.

"WHO ARE YOU?" demanded Tyson Trowel.

"I am the girl's father, sir!" replied the man as he opened his arms to scoop his daughter off. "This is all my fault. Please forgive me. I wanted Stacey to do well so I swapped the CDs. Please, please, please don't blame her!"

"Daddy! You ruined it for me!"

screamed Stacey. She then pinched her father's nose.

"Ouch!" yelled the man.

The audience all booed again.

"BOO!"

"OH, SHUT YOUR FACES!" she bawled

at them, and they booed

even louder this time.

"BOO!"

"Stacey, *please*," pleaded the girl's father. "I just didn't want you to be laughed at."

"Laughed at!" The girl couldn't believe her ears. "Stacey Clog is the greatest singer the world has ever known!"

"BOO!"

Sensing this was great entertainment, and brilliant for ratings, Tyson Trowel spoke up.

"Audience, please. Shut up!"

The audience obeyed him.

"Now, sorry, what's your name again?"

"STACEY CLOG!"

"Stacey Clog, why don't you sing for us without any musical accompaniment?"

"No!" pleaded her father.

"YES!" replied Stacey. "This is the moment that will be remembered forever as the birth of a superstar."

"Excellent!" murmured Tyson, rubbing his hands in glee.

The girl took a deep breath. Her father winced and put his fingers in his ears.

Immediately, a sound so unbearable that you would rather spend eternity being given a wedgie than listen to one more second of it filled the theatre. "ARGH!" screamed the audience.

The noise was so horrendous that Tyson Trowel's wig flew off. PING!

The girl, as always, just carried on. Stacey hit a particularly high note.

"Laaaaaaa

"Laaaaaaa

"Laaaaa

It was so piercingly high that a crack
shot across the ceiling of the theatre.

CRACK!

A giant chandelier
fell to the floor.

SMASH!

The walls started
wobbling...

...!"

...!"

a...!" WOBBLE!

"Laaaaaaa...!"

The audience screamed and ran for their lives...

Tyson desperately tried to find his wig, and was crushed beneath tonnes of debris.

"NOOO!"

Dust was thrown up in the air as if there had been an actual explosion. **Whoosh!**

All of this was captured live on television, until people's TV screens turned black as the cameras were destroyed.

"ARGH!"

...before the entir theatre collapsed

CRASH

It was a momentous night in the history of entertainment. One that would never, ever be forgotten.

So Stacey's dream did come true. The girl became wildly famous. Though for being the worst singer in the world rather than the best. The only positive note was that Stacey had hospitalised Tyson Trowel, and he couldn't be on TV for a whole week.

Although the theatre had completely collapsed, and there were thousands of tonnes of rubble, Father refused to give up the search for his daughter.

After days and nights of digging with his bare hands, he finally found her.

"STACEY!"

the man exclaimed, tears in his eyes.

The girl's dress had been ripped to shreds, her mouth was dry with dust and she was covered from head to toe in dirt. When the man tearfully dragged his daughter out of the rubble, her first words were...

"Did I get through to the next round?"

Fussy
FRANKIE

FRANKIE WAS FUSSY. The little boy refused to eat any fruit or vegetables whatsoever.

If any found their way on to his dinner plate, he would get rid of them immediately. Brussels sprouts would be flicked across the kitchen.

Broccoli would be flung over his shoulder.

Tomatoes would be splatted on the ceiling. Aubergines would be thrown back at whoever had the misfortune of serving them up.

Rhubarb was the boy's absolute worst nightmare. Like a lot of fussy eaters, he'd never actually tasted the food he **hated** the most, but to Frankie it looked and smelled "*yucksome*". Whenever he came face to face with a piece of rhubarb, he took great pleasure in flushing it down the toilet.

"Goodbye, ranky danky rhubarb! Good riddance! Ha! Ha!" the boy would say as he watched it swirl down the pan.

Every morning at breakfast-time in the kitchen Frankie's mum would plead with him. "You need to eat your five a day, Frankie!" The pair lived in a little house on the far side of town. Casting a shadow over the family home was a huge nuclear power station that glowed in the dark and HUMMED all day and night.

"Ma, I do get me five a day!" snapped the boy. "Crisps, biscuits, chocolate, cake and biscuits."

"You counted biscuits twice!"

"Dat's cos I 'ave two packets a day! Duh!"

Frankie's daily menu looked like this:

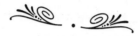

BREAKFAST:
a bowl of crisps with ice cream on top

· · ·

MID-MORNING SNACK:
sweets sprinkled with sugar

· · ·

LUNCH, MAIN COURSE:
a packet of chocolate biscuits
dipped in chocolate sauce

PUDDING:
a deep-fried cake

AFTERNOON TEA:

a packet of double-chocolate biscuits,

washed down with a glass of treacle

...

DINNER, MAIN COURSE:

a chocolate egg on a bed of crisps

PUDDING:

a block of fudge smothered in

fudge sauce

...

BEDTIME SNACK:

a bag of toffees to chew on

The boy's mum was sick with worry about her son. Because of his terrible diet, Frankie was becoming bigger, paler and spottier by the day. So Mum had decided to create a **food revolution** in her house.

Her son was going to eat fresh fruit and vegetables at every meal whether he liked it or not.

THE VEGETABLES ARE COMING

"I'm starvin'. Wot's for brekkie, Ma? If it's not chocolate, then I am puttin' meself up for adoption."

"It's better than chocolate! Just you wait and see."

The lady then whisked out a plate she'd been hiding under a tea towel.

"Ta-da!" she exclaimed excitedly.

"Wot's dis, Ma?" Frankie demanded.

"It's a grapefruit."

"A wotfruit?"

"A grapefruit. It's really delicious. Have a try."

Frankie looked at the thing with contempt. He leaned his face down and took a sniff of it.

"EURGH! IT'S PONKY PONGY!"

"It smells fresh."

"It smells disgustable. I ain't eatin' dat, you cruel old hagwitch! Gimme some chocolate. Now."

The lady was hurt by her son's outburst, but tried to stay strong. "No," she replied.

Frankie couldn't believe his ears. "Wot do ya mean, 'no'? I want chocolate!"

"No, Frankie. Grapefruits are yummy. I promise you.

They taste sweet, just like a... sweet. Come on now. Be a good boy."

The lady tried to feed her son a segment with a spoon as if he was a baby. He struggled for a while, but Mum persevered and eventually got the piece of fruit in her son's mouth. As soon as she had, he spat it back at her.

SPLAT!

It hit the boy's mum right on the nose.

"EURGH!" screamed Frankie. "That tasted like pukey plops!"

As the poor lady peeled the piece of grapefruit from her nose, she realised she might have to try a different approach with her son.

Bribery.

"Look, Frankie," she began, "if you eat the grapefruit, you can have one square of **chocolate** from this giant bar here!"

Mum always had a giant bar of **chocolate** on standby in case her son became angry.

The boy was craving **chocolate**. He hadn't had any for a matter of hours. However, there was no way he was going to eat that y^uc^ky m^uc^ky fruit *thingummy* whatever it was called. A wicked plan crossed his mind.

"All right, Ma, you are right. I should 'ave me five a day. I'll eat it!"

"GOOD BOY!" exclaimed Mum. "Oh, Frankie, I am so pleased! Go ahead th—"

"Nah!" he snapped. "Ya need to get the chocolate out first."

"Yes, yes, of course."

As soon as Mum had turned round, Frankie picked up the grapefruit and h u r l e d it out of the window.

WHOOSH!

It flew right at the nuclear power station.

The grapefruit must have hit something as the lights on the power station *flickered* for a moment.

Mum then turned back with the square of **chocolate** in her hand.

"You finished it!"

"Yeah, Ma!" lied Frankie.

The lady inspected his bowl. "You ate the skin as well."

"Did I?"

"Yes! It's very tough, the skin of a grapefruit."

"Yes, well, that's the best bit, Ma.

Now gimme dat chocolate! Now!

"I said gimme dat chocolate! **Now**!"

The lady was about to hand her son a square of chocolate when he ate it out of her hand like a dog.

"OW!" screamed Mum. "You bit my finger!"

"It was in the way, Ma! Now, what's next?"

Feeling she was on a roll after Frankie had eaten up his grapefruit, skin and all, she tried the next fruit.

A banana.

It was the same routine. Frankie tricked his mum into thinking he'd eaten it in exchange for another square of chocolate. Again the banana was flung out of the window. However, because it was bent, the banana returned to him

like a boomerang, banging

Frankie on the head. So he threw it again, underarm this time, and once again

it hit the power station. The hum
became a loud **grinding** noise.

Mum turned back to see the plate was empty.

"Frankie! You ate the banana skin!"

"Yeah, Ma. It were *yummytastic!* Chocolate! Now!"

"Yes, yes. Of course!"

This time the lady wasn't taking any chances
with her fingers. She had become attached to
them. So she threw the square of chocolate up
into the air for her son to catch in his
mouth, the way one might throw a
fish to a killer whale.

Having had incredible
success with the grapefruit
and banana, the lady thought
it time to become more
adventurous.

So this morning's breakfast was to be
rounded off with an exotic fruit.

A pineapple.

Once again Frankie managed to convince
his mum that he had eaten it whole, when he
had lobbed it out of the window. Once again

it reached the power station,
causing some kind of siren to go
off in there.

"What a super breakfast, Frankie!" said Mum brightly.

"We are on a roll now."

A little later that day it was time for
lunch. Frankie's mum felt she should
try her son on some vegetables. A
cauliflower was the first one to be
flung out of the window as soon as
Mum's back was turned. He threw it like one might
throw a shot put. The boy was given another square
of **chocolate**.

Next a platoon of peas was flicked one by one

off the boy's plate.

PING! PING! PING!

They all flew out of the window straight towards the power station. This was fun!

And the reward was more **chocolate!**

Pudding was a pear. The weird, misshapen, easily bruised apple-type thing was, of course, flung out of the window, and it disappeared somewhere inside the **POWER STATION**.

Mum was worried that because her son was being so good eating up all his fruit and vegetables she was soon going to run out of **chocolate**. The giant bar was very nearly gone.

Dinner was a cabbage. This is a vegetable even people who like vegetables don't like. Even other vegetables shun the cabbage and won't be friends with it.

Cabbage is a vegetable that gives other vegetables a **bad** name.

Yet as soon as his mum's back was turned to break off another square of **chocolate** Frankie appeared to gobble up the whole cabbage in one go.

Really it too had been launched out of the window, once again landing somewhere in the power station, which was now giving off

red **hot** **heat.**

By this time Mum was beginning to become suspicious.

"I hadn't even cooked that cabbage yet!" she exclaimed.

"I like it raw, Ma. More nurtri... nutti... **nunti...**"

The boy was searching for the word "nutritious", but couldn't find it anywhere in his brain, so settled for something simpler. "More fings in it, innit?"

Mum wasn't exactly sure what her son meant, but nodded anyway. "Yes. Good boy."

"CHOCOLATE!"

"Yes, yes, of course! Coming right up!"

For pudding Mum had planned to feed her son his most dreaded food... rhubarb.

"Now, Frankie, let's see what a good boy you really can be! If you eat your rhubarb, you can have two squares of **chocolate**. In fact, you can finish off the whole bar!"

As she turned round to pick up the bar, Mum noticed the window was w i d e open.

"That power station is very hot today," she said to herself, before shutting the window. A piece of rhubarb flew past her head at speed.

WHOOSH!

It bounced off the pane of glass.

BOING!

And struck the lady on her face.

SPLAT!

"Frankie! What on earth do you think you are doing?" demanded Mum. She was furious at having been fooled like this.

"I fink dat rhubarb fingy is still alive! As soon as I bit into it, it ran off!"

"Did it indeed?!"

"Yeah! It ran across the table, then did this big leap fing off it to the window!"

Mum stared at the boy. She was fuming. Frankie knew the game was up. He hadn't seen that look since he'd swapped the family dog for a bag of **fudge**.

"You haven't eaten a single fruit or vegetable I have served up all day, have you?"

Frankie was silent for a moment. "Yeah, I 'ave, Ma."

"Really?"

"Yeah. I took a nibble out of one."

"Which one?"

"A pea."

"You ate ONE pea?"

"Nah, I ate about 'alf of one. It was **ranky danky doodah!** Totally disgustable! Repolting! Never again. Right, Ma, gimme the rest of that choccy bar. NOW!"

"There will be no chocolate for you, young man!" cried Mum. Being called "young man" meant he was in serious trouble. "Now, you get off to bed at once!"

"But, Ma!"

"BED!"

Frankie shrugged and sloped off upstairs to his bedroom. He muttered something about "not caring", but he did really. Nobody wanted to go to bed at six o'clock. Even babies were allowed to stay up later than that.

Frankie harrumphed to himself as he slumped down on his bed. He stared out of the window. It was still light. Something strange was going on at the **nuclear power station**. Red lights were **flashing** everywhere, and workers were running around in what looked like a panic.

"BED! NOW!" shouted Mum from the boy's bedroom door. As he slid under the covers, she drew the curtains. "Tomorrow we are going to start all over again."

"WOT?!"

"Guess what's for breakfast?"

"Dunno. Some'ink *vomiticious* and all *fruityvegetably* I bet."

"You are dead right, young man. **Rhubarb!**"

"NAH!" the boy bawled.

"YES! Rhubarb for breakfast!"

With that, Mum stormed out of the boy's bedroom, dramatically **slamming** the door as she did so.

BANG!

The lady then had a sit-down in a darkened room. She couldn't remember ever being so angry.

That night Frankie found it hard to sleep. The thought of having to eat rhubarb for breakfast made his stomach turn. He tossed and turned for hours, before finally drifting off.

"zZZZ... ZZZZ..."

The sound of someone or something tapping on the window woke him.

TAP! TAP!

Frankie's eyes opened in terror.

Was this one of those dreams where you dream you are awake?

TAP! TAP!

There it was again.

TAP! TAP!

Again.

The boy was shaking with fear. Who or what was out there? His bedroom was on the top floor of the house. It was too high up for anyone to reach.

TAP! TAP!

There was only one thing for it. Frankie would have to peek out of the window. He slid out of bed as quietly as he could, and pulled the curtain back the tiniest bit.

"ARGH!" screamed the boy.

Outside was some kind of monster. It looked like a cabbage, but was about a thousand times the size and was glowing a luminous green colour.

It t^app^ed on the window with its leafy hand.

TAP! TAP!

As it wasn't going away, Frankie slowly opened the curtains. What was this creature?

A giant alien plant from outer space?

"FRANKIE?" it boomed.

The thing knew his name.

"Y-y-yeah?" he stammered.

"FRANKIE, THE FUSSIEST CHILD IN THE WORLD?"

"I guess so. Who are you?"

"I am the cabbage you so cruelly threw out of the window! Yes, we fruits and vegetables do have feelings, you know."

"Why are you all big and talkin'?"

"You threw me so high I went down the chimney of the power station and ended up in the nuclear reactor."

"WOT?" The boy couldn't believe his ears.

Behind the giant cabbage Frankie could see that smoke was billowing from the power station. It was clear the place was going into meltdown.

"Now it's time to get my revenge. If you won't eat me, I will eat you!"

With that, the cabbage's leafy hand smashed through the window and grabbed the boy by the arm.

"OW!" he screamed.

Frankie wrestled free and rushed out of his bedroom.

He raced down the stairs and out into the street. He ran as fast as his legs could carry him. Soon he was out of breath and had a stitch. A diet of cake, crisps, biscuits and chocolate had left the boy unfit.

Limping down the road, Frankie didn't dare look back. Behind him he could hear a **thundering** sound. After a few more steps the boy couldn't help himself. He just had to look back.

At the front was the giant glowing cabbage.

"GET HIM!"

it boomed as it bounced along.

Behind the cabbage was a huge glowing white-and-green thing. It was hopping down the road.

"NASTY LITTLE RUNT!" it shouted. **"LET'S DIGEST HIM SLOWLY! MAKE HIM SUFFER!"**

Next to the humongous cauliflower were a hundred bouncing green spheres. They were about the size of beach balls.

Frankie realised these must be the peas that he had flicked out of the window.

The peas seemed to be crying. "I CAN'T BELIEVE HE DID THIS TO US!" one said, fighting back the tears.

"EVERYONE LIKES PEAS!"

"I don't! Peas are puketastic!" shouted Frankie.

"LET'S TEACH HIM A LESSON!" cried another pea.

"**YES!**" shouted a chorus of them.

The fruits were not to be outdone by the vegetables. A giant grapefruit, a ginormous banana, a colossal pear and an enormous pineapple were all following close behind.

"**KEEP UP!**" said the grapefruit.

"**I AM KEEPING UP, DEAR!**" hissed the pear. "**YOU KNOW I BRUISE EASILY!**"

"**ME TOO!**" chimed in the banana.

The pineapple was pushing past them all to get at the boy.

"OUT OF THE WAY, COMMONERS! EXOTIC FRUIT COMING THROUGH!"

it bellowed in a posh voice.

Frankie was frozen in fear. The fruits and vegetables surrounded him, all ready to pounce. "Please! Please! I beg you! Don't eat me! I **promise** I'll eat me five a day!"

Just then a voice came from far off. It was a ginormous rhubarb.

"THE BOY IS MINE!"

boomed the rhubarb from the roof of the house.
The vegetable was lit from behind by a silvery moon.

"**WHAT?**" demanded the cabbage.

Frankie looked at the tall pink vegetable thing.

"I didn't even manage to fling ya out the window!" the boy protested. "Ya b⁰uⁿceᵈ off the glass and hit me ma in the face."

"I know," replied the rhubarb. "That is a crime not just against me, but against rhubarbs of the world. I had to avenge them. So I crawled across the kitchen floor, leaped through the cat flap and jumped over the fence to get inside the power station. From there I found my way into the nuclear reactor. BINGO! A nuclear rhubarb! YOUR WORST NIGHTMARE!"

With that the monstrous vegetable leaped off the roof of the house. It flew through the air,

opening its mouth wide, revealing its terrifying rhubarby teeth.

"ARGH!"

screamed the boy as his head was munched off.

All the fruits and vegetables pounced.
"I want an arm!"
shouted the cabbage.

"**I want a leg!**"
exclaimed
the cauliflower.

"*Save us the rest!*"
said the fruits.

It was a feeding frenzy. The boy was gone in seconds. The peas b^{ou}nced up and gobbled down what was left of him.

That was the end of Fussy Frankie.

So, children, please remember this important lesson...

Eat your greens, or one day they might **eat you.**

Cruel
CLARISSA

PRETTY

PINK

POISONOUS

Cruel
CLARISSA

ONCE THERE LIVED a girl called Clarissa. On the outside she appeared to be the sweetest, kindest, gentlest little girl you could ever meet. Clarissa would wear little old-fashioned **pink** dresses, always with matching **pink** ribbons in her hair.

Everything in her bedroom was a shade of **pink.**

Clarissa had **pink** teddy bears,

pink ponies and a **pink** vanity set.

The only colouring crayons
she had were shades of **pink**.

The girl had a collection of
antique porcelain dolls all
dressed in **pink** nightdresses
that she tucked up in bed
with her when she went to sleep.

Clarissa's favourite toy was
a miniature **pink** tea set.

She would delight her grandmas and grandads by letting them watch her drink tea from a tiny cup and stuff her face with dozens of fairy cakes with **pink** icing. Everyone thought the little girl was absolutely adorable.

However, this delightful behaviour masked what Clarissa was really like. The girl had a streak of dire cruelty within her.

A cruelty towards cats.*

When she was a baby, Clarissa had grabbed a cat's tail and yanked it as hard as she could.

"MIAOW!"

The creature had hissed at the baby and made her cry. Ever since then she'd hated the animals, and whenever no one was looking she would do something beastly to a cat.

Clarissa would pour pepper into a cat's food so it had a **sneezing** fit.

Atishoo!

---

* Cruelty to any animals is wicked, something I know you would never, ever do!

Squeeze glue on to the branches of a tree so cats would get stuck up there.

Tie two cats' tails together so neither could go anywhere.

Paint one bright **pink** so it looked like a stick of candyfloss.

Attach one to a kite and then launch the terrified creature into the air.

She would stick a stamp on one, and post it to Australia.

Use a hundred remote-controlled toy mice to drive a cat crazy.

Swap one with her grandma's wig so the cat would be plonked on top of the old lady's head all day.

Clarissa had been tormenting the local cats like this for years. But she'd never had one of her own.

As it was her birthday coming up, Clarissa asked her parents for a very special present.

"Mama! Papa?" The little girl spoke in a *singsong* voice to make herself seem sweet.

"Yes, my angel sent from heaven?" replied Papa.

"I am an *ikkle* bit lonely."

"Oh, my sweet ***babycakes***!" said Mama.

"Whatever can we do, my *snowflake*?"

"Mama, Papa. It would be awfully nice if I had an *ikkle kitten* to..."

What was she going to say?

"...love."

The girl's parents had tears in their eyes. She had fooled them good and proper.

"How did we create a child so **perfect**?" asked Mama.

"Clarissa is **better** than **perfect**," replied Papa.

The little girl smirked to herself.

Mama and Papa couldn't wait until Clarissa's birthday, which was a whole week away, so the very next morning they surprised her with a special present. Mama and Papa took Clarissa up her breakfast tray as they always did. The girl had breakfast served to her in bed every morning. But, when they lifted the silver cover off the platter, instead of boiled eggs and soldiers there was the **cutest kitten** you have ever seen.

"*Surprise!*" said Mama and Papa.

The kitten's fur was as white as snow. It had the biggest, bluest eyes, the softest paws, and a kissable nose that was **dinky** and *pinky* in colour.

As Mama handed it to her, the little girl scooped it up in her arms and held it tight. The kitten miaowed in pleasure and snuggled up to her.

"MIAOW!"

"Mama, Papa! I **love** her!"

exclaimed Clarissa.

"And she is going to love you!" replied Papa.

"To the moon and back!" added Mama. "What are you going to call her?"

Clarissa thought for a moment. *"Blossom!"*

"Oh, my most darling of darlings, that's the sweetest name I've ever heard," gushed Mama.

"They are both so adorable together I want to weep," announced Papa.

"Happy tears I hope, Papa?" asked Mama.

"Tears of pure joy," replied Papa.

"Good. Now Blossom is all yours, my sweetest sugar-drop, so promise me you'll take good care of her?" asked Mama.

"Of course I will. And I just want to say you are the best papa and mama in the world, and I love you heaps and heaps."

Mama and Papa looked at each other, *beaming with pride*, and left the room.

As soon as the door had closed, the little girl's cuter-than-cute expression changed.

"Right, Blossom!" Clarissa snarled. Her voice was **deeper** now, and the cutesy singsong tone had vanished.

Immediately the little kitten was shaking with fear.

"Cats are vile creatures. Now I have one to torment to my heart's content!"

"MIAOW!"

cried Blossom.

The first thing that Cruel Clarissa did was put headphones over the kitten's ears and make her listen to a **booming** Beethoven symphony really **loud**.

BA BA BA BOM! BA BA BA BOM!

The little girl laughed...

"Ha! Ha! Ha!"

...as poor Blossom suffered.

"MIAOW!"

Clarissa flung Blossom on to the fan hanging from the ceiling in her bedroom and put the speed up as high as it would go. "MIAOW!"

She mixed chilli powder in with the cat food. That meant when the kitten broke wind she shot up into the air.

PPPFFFTTT!!!

"MIAOW!"

The girl put her hair
in curlers and gave Blossom
an awful perm.

"MIAOW!"

Like a pirate, Clarissa made
Blossom walk the plank into the pond.

PLOP!

"MIAOW!"

She styled her whiskers so it looked as if she had the
silly moustache made famous by Spanish surrealist
painter Salvador Dalí.

"WOOF!"

Worst of all was the time Clarissa smuggled
Blossom into the Crufts dog show under her
coat and then let the poor creature loose for
the dogs to chase.

"WOOF!"

"WOOF!"

Now, of course, cats are very intelligent beings.
If you look at a list of animals from

Orang-utan

Dolphin

Elephant

Cat

to **stupidest,**

you will see that cats come near the top:

Goldfish

Slug

Sponge

Crow

Bear

Human

One night while Clarissa was sleeping in her little pink bed after yet another long day of kitten-tormenting, Blossom just managed to squeeze herself out of an open window. The kitten hopped across the roofs of neighbouring houses, and followed the sound of distant miaows. Blossom found a garden where the local cats were all having their nightly meeting.

Under the *silvery glow of the moon*, the animals were dealing with business. Cat business. There were squabbles over territories, reports of badly behaved

dogs and tales shared of which old ladies were kindest by putting out saucers of milk for them.

Overseeing it all was a **mangy** old tomcat who lived wild on a rubbish dump. Little Blossom was nervous about joining the group at first, but eventually she jumped down off the roof and met her fellow felines. Through tears, Blossom told the other cats about the cruelty she suffered at the hands of her owner. Needless to say, the cats were **furious**. How could anyone treat a defenceless little kitten like that?

"MIAOW!"

Once Blossom had described Clarissa to them, it turned out that they'd all been victims of this beastly child too.

As leader of the coven of cats, the tomcat announced that they would all work together to take revenge on Cruel Clarissa. With a show of paws the motion was passed. The very next night under the cover of darkness the cats would strike.

The following morning Clarissa woke up with just one thing on her mind. Kitten-punishing.

The girl strapped Blossom to a roller-skate and propelled her down the stairs.

CLUNK!
CLUNK!
CLUNK!

Clarissa pegged the poor creature to the washing line right between Papa's underpants and Mama's frilly knickers.

$\mathcal{S}WING!$

Clarissa tied the kitten to a model railway track, then flicked a switch to drive a train towards her at speed.

WHIRR!

She attached a home-made contraption to the kitten's back, which dangled a budgerigar in a cage in front of her face, just out of reach.

"TWEET! TWEET!"

Clarissa painted all of Blossom's fur blue and placed a white sock on her head to make her look like a Smurf.

Finally Clarissa ate ten tins of baked beans and blew off **violently** right on top of the kitten's head.

TRUMPETY
TRUMP
TRUMP
TRUMP!

However, despite all this kitten-bothering today, Blossom didn't look the least bit bothered.

In fact, throughout all these ordeals the kitten just purred away.

Blossom knew what was coming as soon as night fell.

"Just you wait until tomorrow, Blossom!

Ha

ha!"

whispered the girl menacingly. She went to bed dreaming of more ways she could make her kitten suffer. "ZzZzzzZZZZZ!"

In the middle of the night the girl was woken up by a foul smell. She realised there was something whiffy right in front of her nose. Opening one eye, she saw a little furry face staring back at her. Opening her other eye, Clarissa realised the terrible truth.

She was staring straight at a cat's bottom.
No wonder it was whiffy! It belonged to the dirty old tomcat.

"Argh!" Clarissa screamed. The girl tried to get up, but couldn't move. Looking down at her arms and legs she realised they were covered in cats. All these strange moggies were pinning her down.

"GET OFF ME, YOU VILE CREATURES!" she screamed, but the cats wouldn't let go. The girl flailed her arms and legs around, but still they wouldn't let go. Using all her might, Clarissa rolled herself off her bed.

T
H
U
M
P!

With great difficulty, she stood up. Catching a glimpse of herself in the mirror, to her horror Clarissa realised she was covered from head to toe in cats. Sitting on top of her head was Blossom herself. The kitten was smiling and purring loudly.

"PURR! PURR!"
This was REVENGE!

The girl tried to knock the cats off by banging her arms and legs against the furniture in her bedroom, but the creatures just dug their sharp claws into her and clung on all the more. "OW!" yelled the girl.

There was nothing for it. Clarissa had to scare the cats off herself. One thing these animals hated was water, so the girl raced down the stairs and across the back garden in the direction of the pond. She took a running jump. Seeing the water ahead, the cats all dived off her and on to the ground.

SPLOSH!

Cruel Clarissa landed in the pond.

After a moment she popped her head up out of the **cold, green water**, weeds stuck to her hair. The cats gathered around the pond. They hissed at her fiercely and reached out their paws to swipe her.

"HISS!"

So the girl ducked her head under the water again and held her breath. Surely the cats would disperse. But when she resurfaced they were still there.

"HISS!"

Again the outstretched paws all **swiped** towards her, their claws out.

Clarissa hid underwater again.

This went on all night.

As dawn broke, her parents ran into the garden and shooed the cats away.

"SHOO!"

Blossom jumped on to the back of the old tomcat, and they all darted off.

Mama and Papa dragged their daughter out of the water.

"My poor darling!" cried Mama. "What on earth has happened to our little ray of sunshine?"

The girl had turned a nasty shade of green, and was shivering with the cold.

"BRrrr!"

Her teeth were chattering like crazy.

CHATTER! CHATTER! *CHATTER!*

A frog was crouched on top of her head.

"Ribbit!"

Clarissa coughed and spluttered, and a tadpole she had swallowed shot out of her mouth.

PING!

"WHAAA!" she wailed. The girl had never felt so sorry for herself in all her life.

Cruel Clarissa had learned her lesson. **She would never, ever** torment a cat **again.**

The tomcat took Blossom off to a lovely family, who had often fed the old stray fish and chips. There Blossom stayed, loved by everyone.

For her next birthday Clarissa begged her parents for a very different present.

"Mama? Papa?" said the girl.

"Yes, my **scrumptious** little fairy cake?" replied Mama.

"Please can I have an ikkle bunny?"

HARRY,

Who Never, Ever Did His Homework

HARRY HATED HOMEWORK. He did everything he could to avoid doing it.

The boy had a long list of excuses he would recite to teachers explaining why he couldn't hand it in:

My goldfish ate it.

My mum ate it. She's been on a diet and was extremely peckish.

The house was robbed by a gang of burglars and the first thing they took was my Geography exercise book. There is a big criminal black market in Geography homework.

My homework was deemed so superb that it went straight to the British Library, where it will be kept under glass for future generations.

I left it on the back seat of my dad's car, but unfortunately a hippopotamus escaped from the zoo and sat on the car, destroying everything inside.

My little sister is an **origami master** and used the pages of my exercise book to make a huge paper re-creation of Ancient Tokyo.

It was put in a **rocket** and blasted into space by **NASA scientists** attempting to seek contact with aliens to show there is intelligent life on Earth

We were all out of loo paper, so my Aunt Rose used it to wipe her bottom.

It was struck by a **bolt of lightning** and it burst into a ball of flames.

Secret Service agents confiscated it as they said it contained a top-secret algebra equation.

$$2x^3 + 128y^3 = 2\left(x^3 + 64y^3\right)$$

Because Harry never, ever did his homework, he had time to do all the fun things he wanted to do after school, like play on his games console for hours and hours, and... Actually, that's it. Playing computer games was all the boy liked doing. If he had his way, he would play computer games all day and all night. His thumbs working the controller, the boy would laugh to himself...

"Ha! Ha! Ha!"

...as he thought about all his classmates having to do their homework while he drove racing cars through the streets of Monte Carlo, or flew through space shooting lasers, or scored the winning goal in the World Cup.

The boy had **not** handed in his homework for so many years that his teachers had all given up on him.

However, one day a new teacher arrived at the school, a *mysterious* old History teacher, called Madame Magna. This lady was dressed from head to toe in **black**, with a lace scarf covering her head, which all but obscured her eyes.

Madame Magna smelled like an old, musty book that you might find in a jumble sale, and she spoke with a funny accent that nobody could quite place. Rumours about the old lady swirled around the school. On her arrival some children thought she might be a witch.

Others thought she was a time traveller who had actually lived through all these moments in history that she taught. Guesses about her age ranged from **seventy** to **seven hundred**.

Even the other teachers kept their distance from her. At lunchtime, Madame Magna sat alone under a tree smoking a long pipe.

The plumes of smoke would float in the air and swirl into the shapes of people or animals.

Madame Magna turned pipe-smoking into an art.

Our story begins on the day Harry had his first lesson with the new teacher. Madame Magna was teaching the children all about the various methods of medieval torture. As the bell rang, Harry was the first to leap up out of his chair to go.

"*Homevork* in first thing tomorrow!" announced Madame Magna. "Harry, vould you stay behind, PLEASE?"

Harry let out a huge sigh. "What now, miss?"

"Madame!"

"What now, madame?"

"It has come to my attention that you have never vonce handed in your *homevork*!"

"Well, miss, I mean madame..." began Harry. He was very experienced at giving teachers the brush-off with some ridiculous excuse, so was not too worried. "That is strange, because I did it all.

Maybe the WORDS JUST FELL OFF THE PAGES

in my exercise book?"

Madame Magna took out her pipe and stuffed the end with tobacco. Slowly she lit it with a match, and blew a huge cloud of foul-smelling smoke into the boy's face. Harry coughed and spluttered as the smoke swirled around him. The boy was sure he could see shapes of knights in armour on horseback jousting in the smoke. However, no sooner had he seen the vision than it was gone.

"Vell, vell, vell, Harry, you are quite the joker! But if you **don't** do your *homevork* tonight, you may be visited by

apparitions in the dead of night."

The boy was unnerved by this. "What do you mean, miss, er, madame?"

"You *vill* see for yourself. You are the master of your destiny."

"Can I go now, miss-madame?"

"Yes." The old lady took another long drag on her pipe, and blew a huge, **thick** cloud of smoke right in the direction of the boy. This time he was sure he could see camels and slaves and the pyramids of Ancient Egypt.

Harry coughed and spluttered again. When the smoke had cleared, she was gone.

Harry was seriously spooked.

What did the mysterious madame mean by "apparitions in the dead of night"?

The boy ran all the way home, and as soon as he was in his bedroom he rummaged in his school bag for his History exercise book. It was all but empty of work.

HARRY, WHO NEVER, EVER DID HIS HOMEWORK

Harry had been doodling instead of making notes for most of the term.

The History homework, or "*homevork*", that Madame Magna had set for the evening was an essay: **"Who is the greatest villain in the history of the *vorld?*"** (Harry realised the teacher meant "world".)

The boy ponderd the question for a while. The problem was he hadn't listened to a word, or even a *vord,* she had said in class, so Harry hadn't the faintest idea who to write about. The boy knew that Darth Vader was a villain, but was pretty sure that he'd been made up, rather than being a figure from world history.

Harry scratched his head. Then he chewed his pen. Then he picked his nose. He did lots of things other than his homework. In no time, he had discarded his

exercise book and was back playing on his games console, saving the galaxy or destroying the galaxy or some such nonsense.

When Harry finally went to bed, he'd forgotten all about his History homework, and the teacher's strange premonition. After **hours** of playing computer games, the boy was tired and went straight to sleep.

A **deathly chill** passed through his room in the middle of the night.

It woke Harry up. Opening his eyes, he saw that a huge cloud of silky grey smoke had filled the room. The smoke was *swirling and twirling* into shapes, and finally settled to create five terrifying figures, all in historical clothing.

"Who are you?" demanded the boy.

"We are the greatest villains in history," said one in a suit of

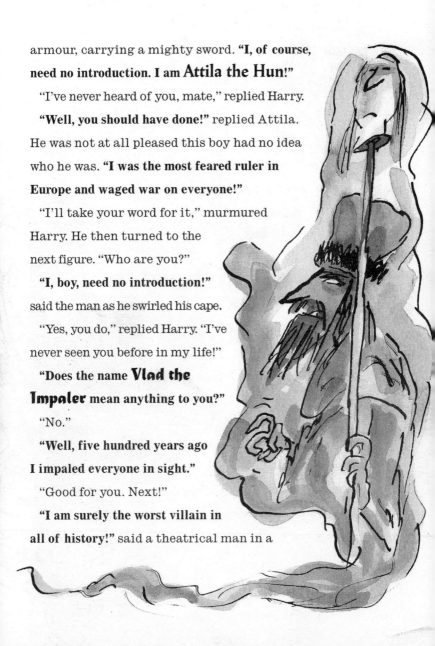

armour, carrying a mighty sword. **"I, of course, need no introduction. I am Attila the Hun!"**

"I've never heard of you, mate," replied Harry.

"Well, you should have done!" replied Attila. He was not at all pleased this boy had no idea who he was. **"I was the most feared ruler in Europe and waged war on everyone!"**

"I'll take your word for it," murmured Harry. He then turned to the next figure. "Who are you?"

"I, boy, need no introduction!" said the man as he swirled his cape.

"Yes, you do," replied Harry. "I've never seen you before in my life!"

"Does the name Vlad the Impaler mean anything to you?"

"No."

"Well, five hundred years ago I impaled everyone in sight."

"Good for you. Next!"

"I am surely the worst villain in all of history!" said a theatrical man in a white robe with a crown of gold leaves on top of his head.

"So what's your name?"

"**Caligula! I was Emperor of the Roman Empire. But, more than that, A GOD!**"

"**Oh, here he goes again...**" muttered Attila.

"**But I murdered far more people!**" said a flamboyantly dressed figure in a white wig.

"**Let me introduce myself, child, as you clearly are something of an ignoramus. I am** *Robespierre*, **the leader of the French Revolution. I executed thousands of people, including some of my closest friends.**"

"Why did you do that?" asked Harry. "If you didn't like them, then why not just never text them back? After a while, they'd have got the message."

"This was the 1790s! We didn't have mobile telephones then, you buffoon!"

"Ha! Ha! Ha!" came a voice. Sitting in the corner of Harry's bedroom was a heavy-looking man with a long, grey beard. **"You are all nobodies compared to me!"**

"Who are you?" asked Harry.

"I know you jest with me, child. I am Genghis Khan, ruler of the Mongol Empire. As I swept across the world,

my army killed millions of people. Who cares about a few less Frenchmen? Pah!"

With that, Genghis Khan **SPAT** on the floor. Robespierre was fuming.

"How dare you! Some spit landed on my tights! Wipe it off at once!"

"I will not!" replied Genghis.

"Whoo!" cooed Caligula, mocking them. "Come on now, children, let's not fall out!"

"SHUT UP!"

ordered Harry.

The world's worst villains were stunned into silence. No one had ever told them to shut up before.

"Now, can you please tell me what you are all doing here in my bedroom? I'd rather you didn't kill me, if you don't mind, because I've just got to level eight on my game."

All the villains laughed.

"Kill you?" said Vlad.

"**As if we would do such a thing**," added Genghis.

"So what are you going to do?" demanded Harry.

"**We are going to make you do your homework!**" announced Robespierre.

"Oh no!" replied the boy.

"**Oh yes!**" said Attila.

"Not fair!" said Harry.

All night the villains stood over the boy as he was forced to do his History homework. Just as Harry would write a sentence, a violent argument would break out between the villains.

"**But you can't begin a sentence with 'but'!**" Robespierre bawled.

"**You just did!**" Vlad the Impaler replied, before impaling the leader of the French Revolution.

Slowly but surely the essay began to take shape. The villains were more than happy to give the boy the facts and figures he needed as they boasted about their awful achievements.

"**The guillotine was a very effective way of putting all the French nobility to death!**" Robespierre bragged.

"**How mind-numbingly dull!**" Caligula replied. "**In

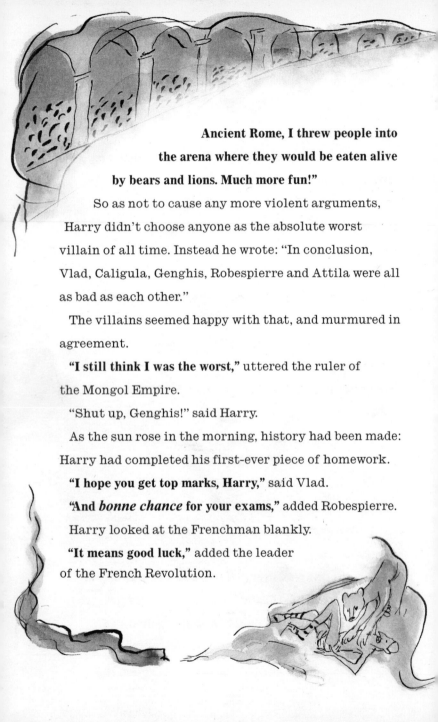

Ancient Rome, I threw people into the arena where they would be eaten alive by bears and lions. Much more fun!"

So as not to cause any more violent arguments, Harry didn't choose anyone as the absolute worst villain of all time. Instead he wrote: "In conclusion, Vlad, Caligula, Genghis, Robespierre and Attila were all as bad as each other."

The villains seemed happy with that, and murmured in agreement.

"I still think I was the worst," uttered the ruler of the Mongol Empire.

"Shut up, Genghis!" said Harry.

As the sun rose in the morning, history had been made: Harry had completed his first-ever piece of homework.

"I hope you get top marks, Harry," said Vlad.

"And *bonne chance* for your exams," added Robespierre.

Harry looked at the Frenchman blankly.

"It means good luck," added the leader of the French Revolution.

"Thank you. I will try."

"Maybe try and do your French homework from now on too."

"Yes, all right!" replied the boy, in a strop.

"You do too much playing on this computer-game doodah," declared Genghis.

"I know," agreed Harry.

"Promise me you will cut down the hours on it," said Caligula.

"I promise," replied the boy.

"Our work here is done, gentlemen, and, of course, Vlad," said Robespierre. ***"Adieu!"***

Just as the villains had appeared in a cloud of smoke, they disappeared in one too.

Despite all their craziness, Harry was going to miss having them around.

Although he'd had a sleepless night, the boy skipped to school in the morning and couldn't wait to hand in his homework to his History teacher.

Madame Magna read it eagerly and was mightily impressed. "This is *vonderful.* Absolutely *vonderful!*" she exclaimed as she puffed on her pipe.

"Thanks, miss, I mean madame."

"Is this all your own vork or did anyone help you vith it?" enquired the teacher with a wry smile.

"I had a tiny bit of help."

"Yes, I know, boy," replied Madame Magna, before blowing a huge plume of smoke into the classroom.

It took the shape of the five most evil villains in history: **Vlad**, Caligula, Genghis, *Robespierre* and **Attila.** They all smiled at Harry.

Just as Madame Magna hobbled off down the corridor, the boy called after her.

"But, just so you know, this whole homework thing was very much a one-off."

The lady stopped and turned back to face Harry.

"Is that so?" she replied.

"Yes. I won't be doing it again."

"*Vot* a shame. And I know you vould so enjoy tonight's *homevork*. It's all about our old friend Boudicca, the Ancient British queen who led the revolt against the Romans."

"Gosh, that sounds sooooo boring."

"Vell, let's hope she doesn't make a little visit tonight in her chariot."

Madame Magna smiled and puffed on her pipe. The corridor was filled with **thick** black smoke. It *swirled* into the shape of a queen riding a chariot pulled by her two powerful horses. The wheels on the chariot had razor-sharp blades.

Blades that could chop YOUR LEGS off in a heartbeat.

The chariot was travelling at enormous speed, and the blades were coming right towards Harry.

"DEATH TO ROMANS!" shouted Boudicca.

The boy was trembling with fear. "All right! All right! I'll do it."

"*Vot* a good boy!" replied Madame Magna.

The lady inhaled on her pipe, and Queen Boudicca vanished. Harry watched as his teacher made her way down the corridor. With every step she became fainter and fainter, until Madame Magna melted into air, into thin air. The teacher disappeared as mysteriously as she had appeared.

From that day on Harry always did his homework. He never wanted to see that terrifying teacher again.

Gruesome
GRISELDA

YUCKY

MUCKY

PLUCKY

Gruesome
GRISELDA

CREEPY-CRAWLIES ARE CALLED CREEPY-CRAWLIES
for a reason. They are creepy and they are crawly.
Slugs, worms, spiders, caterpillars and cockroaches are
creatures that give most people the creeps.

Not Griselda.

GRUESOME GRISELDA

Griselda was a girl who loved creepy-crawlies. If she saw a worm **wiggling** around in the mud, she would pick it up and put it in her pocket.

Now, worms don't make the best pets.

Worms don't come if you call them.

"Worm!"

If you throw a worm a stick, it won't bring it back.

"Worm! Fetch!"

You can't train worms to do tricks.

"Worm! **Roll over!**

Worm! **Beg!**

Worm! **Paw!**"

However, Griselda had other plans for these **slimy** creatures. The little girl would use them to give people the willies.

Griselda attended an incredibly **posh** all-girls boarding school:

THE DUCHESS OF QUEENSBURY'S SCHOOL FOR GIRLS

(with Extremely Wealthy Parents)

The school was full of **young ladies** with long hair and even longer names, like the Honourable Lady Antonia-Rose Huntingdon-Smythe.

They were all more perfect than perfect with their

perfect skin

and perfect teeth

and perfect nails.

In their spare time the girls liked to press wild flowers, embroider lace handkerchiefs and decorate fairy cakes.

Griselda delighted in being the odd one out. The little girl never brushed her hair so it was like a bird's nest, topped off with a **grotty** purple hair scrunchie. She loved having black **grime** under her fingernails. And, most of all, Griselda was proud to be more than a **little pongy**.

The very proper headmistress, Miss Fragrant, would take one look at the girl and **bawl** at her,

"Griselda! You need a bath!"

"No, thank you, Headmistress. Lying in your own **filthy bathwater** for hours can't be healthy!"

Then off Griselda would bound to **roll** in some mud, drag herself through a bush or lie in a **puddle**.

When night fell, Griselda would sneak out of her dormitory to find some **creepy**-crawlies. These she used to play **gruesome** tricks on everyone else at school.

There was the time when the little girl gathered **hundreds of leeches**. She placed them under the covers of the head girl's bed.

A nasty slippery surprise was waiting for Lady Clarissa-Jane Hever-Blenheim when she slid between the sheets.

"ARGH!"

screamed the girl as outside the window Gruesome Griselda sniggered to herself.

"Huh! Huh! Huh!"

Or there was the day when Griselda spied a pair of the headmistress's *frilly bloomers* hanging on the washing line of her garden. Griselda picked up the two **longest, tickliest caterpillars** she could find, and then hid them in the lady's knickers. That morning in assembly as Miss Fragrant was leading the entire school in prayers, the headmistress found herself unable to keep still.

"OOOH!"

Her bottom had never felt so itchy. **"AAAH!"**

All the schoolgirls looked at the lady aghast as the usually proper Miss Fragrant **wriggled** and **hopped** around the stage, **YELPING** like a little dog.

"YAP!
YAP!
YAP!"

Only Griselda knew the reason why. Sitting in the back row of the school hall, she couldn't help smirking at the chaos she had caused.

Worst of all was the time on Prize-giving Day when the guest of honour at the school was none other than

Her Majesty the Queen.

The Queen was there to hand out the prizes to all the girls who were even more *superior* than the others, and give a speech on how best to succeed in life.

When all this was happening, Griselda (who was unlikely to be burdened with any prize, unless there was one for **cheesiest** feet) sneaked off to the school kitchen. There she replaced all the cucumber in the sandwiches with live **slippery slugs**.

As all the prize-winners took tea and sandwiches at the garden party after with the Queen, everyone was on their absolute best behaviour. Even though the cucumber sandwiches tasted disgusting, the teachers, parents and prize-winning girls all swallowed them without complaint. No one wanted to make a scene in the presence of such a distinguished guest.

"Delightful sandwiches," said one old duchess.

"Yes, this cucumber is so fresh-tasting," replied a countess. "It's almost as if it's alive!"

Who would spit out their food in front of Her Majesty the Queen? Well, nobody except Her Majesty the Queen. This was for the simple reason that she was Her Majesty the Queen already. Her Royal Highness took one bite of her slug sandwich and immediately spat it out.

"BLEURGH!"

she screamed as she splattered the food all over the headmistress. Breadcrumbs covered Miss Fragrant's hair while a half-chewed slug ended up stuck to her glasses.

Above their heads a branch of a tree was bouncing

up and down. Griselda was hiding up there, hooting to herself uncontrollably.

"There was a live slug in my sandwich!" barked the Queen.

"Is that so?" replied the headmistress, squirming with embarrassment as all eyes turned to her. "Does Your Royal Highness not like live slugs as a sandwich filling?"

"NO!" replied the Queen. "And not dead ones either."

"Noted! We promise never to serve Your Royal Highness any slug-based snacks next time."

"There won't be a next time!" spluttered

the Queen as she marched off in the direction of her

Rolls-Royce. "Slug sandwiches!
I have been served some
revolting food on my travels,
but this is the absolute worst.
Have that headmistress locked in
a dungeon in the Tower of London!"

"It's a museum now, ma'am," replied her lady-
in-waiting.

"Well, then lock her up in the gift
shop," snapped the Queen. She slumped in the
back of her Rolls-Royce. "Put your foot
down, man!"

"Yes, ma'am!" replied the chauffeur as the beast of a car **ZOOMED** away, the flags flapping in the wind.

"And stop at the nearest kebab shop. I need to have something to take this disgusting taste away!" the Queen barked, desperately trying to rub the **slug juice** off her tongue with a lace handkerchief.

This was the darkest day in the school's long history.

Immediately all the pupils, parents and teachers were gripped by this mystery. Who was the phantom **creepy-crawlies** pest?

WANTED posters were put up all over the school.

WANTED

Do you know who put leeches in the

head girl's bed, hid caterpillars in the

headmistress's undergarments and put an

unspeakable creature in the otherwise

delicious sandwiches served to

Her Majesty the Queen **on Prize-giving Day?**

Information wanted.

£100**0** reward

given for any information that

leads to their capture.

All the girls at Duchess of Queensbury's were too rich
to care about a mere hundred pounds, so the reward
had to be put up to **one thousand pounds**. That was a whole
week's pocket money to some of those girls.

Still there were more attacks.

A toilet bowl in the staffroom was **filled** with **cockroaches**. They nipped the bottom of the History teacher, Miss Wolsley, as soon as she sat on the toilet seat.

"OUCH!"

A huge **hair y** spider gave the Art teacher, Miss Hockney, the **shock** of her life when it was put in her box of brooches and the lady tried to pin it to her chest.

"AAH!"

And the school matron came in for a **nasty surprise** when she poured herself a large tumbler of whisky at the end of the day, only to find the bottle was full of **live maggots**.

"NOOOO!"

GRUESOME GRISELDA

Every time Griselda played a nasty trick on someone, she wanted it to be even more gruesome than the last.

Mornings before school Griselda would rise at dawn to go down to the pond to fish out tadpoles, frogs and newts. Lunchtimes were spent foraging in the grounds for beetles, centipedes and woodlice.

In the dead of night Griselda would sneak out of her bed to dig up the school playing field for worms. Each night she would put hundreds of the wiggliest ones in a wheelbarrow and take them back to her dormitory.

All the creatures would be stored in a huge trunk under the girl's bed. It was a treasure trove of yuck.

Soon the trunk was a swirling, whirling mass of creepy-crawlies.

Griselda would laugh to herself "Ha! Ha! Ha!" as she poured in her latest finds.

When she finally slipped into bed after her foraging expeditions, Griselda would dream up her next nightmare. The bigger, the badder, the better. From out of the darkest corner of her mind crawled the nastiest of thoughts. Could Griselda use all these creatures at once? That way she could create the most gruesome trick of all time. This would be her masterpiece.

It was a gruesome plan, even by Griselda's standards.

The little girl decided she would fill the headmistress's bath from top to bottom with **creepy**-crawlies. Miss Fragrant always lectured Griselda about having a "jolly good soak", and would often rhapsodise to her pupils in assembly on the JOYS of bath-time.

"Girls, you must bathe at least thrice a day. It cleanses not just the body, but more importantly the mind," she would say.

As soon as it went dark, Griselda dragged her heavy trunk to the headmistress's cottage. She climbed into the house through an open window, and found the bathroom. The bath was already full of hot water, and the sweet **smell** of **lavender oil** hung in the air. It was a smell that made Griselda feel sick.

"YUCK!"

The lights in the bathroom were dimmed and candles were placed around the bath. The girl pulled the plug and drained the bath of water. In the next room, she could spy the headmistress in her nightgown putting her long grey hair up into a bath cap in readiness for her nightly **soak**.

Next the gruesome girl put the plug back in and poured all the **creepy-crawlies** from her trunk into the bath. She filled it to the brim.

It was a terrifying sight: all those **creepy-crawlies** creepy-crawling over each other. It was a sea of **horrors**.

Griselda stood back and admired her work.

"Ha! Ha! Ha!"

she sniggered to herself at the **wicked** picture she had painted in her mind of Miss Fragrant unwittingly slipping into the bath.

However, as the little girl was lost in thought, the headmistress swung open the bathroom door.

BANG!

The door knocked Griselda clean over and she **toppled** head first into the bath.

"ARGH!"

In seconds the **creepy-crawlies** covered her. They devoured her instantly. The headmistress desperately tried to pull Griselda out of the bath.

"Griselda!

GRISELDA!"

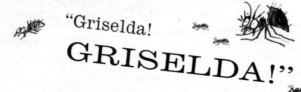

But there was nothing left of the girl, save for a **half-eaten** purple hair scrunchie.

In a way, Griselda had been right. Baths were not for her.

If she had lived, the girl would have learned an important lesson:

NEVER
PLAY TRICKS
ON PEOPLE
THAT YOU
WOULDN'T
WANT PLAYED
ON YOU.

Spoiled
BRAD

BRAD WAS THE most spoiled boy in the world. He came from a super-rich family, who made their money from having money. Brad lived with his mom and pop in a one-hundred-bedroomed mansion in America.

Because Brad was so spoiled, he didn't even take care of the amazing things he was given.

His mom and pop bought their only child all he ever dreamed of and more...

A hundred puppies that Brad quickly tired of and put in the trash.

"WOOF!"

His own miniature **white limousine** that Brad deliberately crashed into a wall at speed, smashing it to pieces.

CRUNCH!

A robot that Brad's mom and pop bought their son to keep him company as he didn't have any friends. Somehow Brad managed to fall out with the robot, and he pushed it into the swimming pool. It lay at the bottom, rusting away.

GURGLE! GURGLE! GURGLE!

A ball-serving machine that was meant to help Brad with his tennis lessons. Instead the boy turned it on his long-suffering tennis coach, firing balls straight at him as if it was a cannon.

"OUCH!"

A complete set of **leather-bound encyclopaedias.** He read the entry for "aardvark" and then gave up and used the rest of the pages as toilet roll.

RIP! WIPE!

A priceless old oil painting that Brad smashed his head through so he could use it as a Halloween costume.

SMASH!

A cut-glass chandelier for his bedroom that he used to swing on.

SWING!

An antique double bass that Brad had never once played. Instead, when the snow came, the boy sat on the instrument to use it as a toboggan.

WHIZZ!

One morning Brad swept down the family mansion's **long** staircase in his *silk pyjamas, dressing gown* and monogrammed ***velvet*** slippers.

"Good morning, Bradley Junior," murmured his parents. Pop was checking his stocks and shares in the *Financial Times*. Meanwhile, Mom was reading a glossy magazine and taking some pleasure in pictures of the **rich and famous** who'd had plastic surgery that had gone horribly wrong. As usual, they were being waited on by their rather **snooty** English butler, Hopkins.

"Pancakes, butler!" demanded the boy as he entered the grand dining room and walked over to the impossibly long table. "With cream, ice cream and chocolate sauce!

Now!"

"Yes, of course, young sir," purred Hopkins, before bowing and retreating to the kitchen.

Brad Junior slumped down at his usual place at the head of the table.

"Mom? Pop?"

"Yes, Bradley Junior? Did you enjoy your million-dollar birthday party yesterday?" asked Pop.

"It was so-so," the boy replied. "I have been thinking."

"Oh yes..." prompted Mom. It wasn't often her son thought.

"It's not fair that I have to wait another whole year for my birthday."

"Well, everyone has to wait, Bradley Junior," said Pop. "That's why birthdays are special."

"I don't want to wait!" declared the boy. "I want it to be my birthday every day!"

Mom and Pop shared a look. They were used to their son acting like a spoiled brat, but this was a new low.

"Son! Yesterday we laid on an *incredibly expensive* day for you," began Mom. "You had a giant chocolate cake..."

"I love cake!" announced Brad.

"We know," said Pop.

"There was a funfair in the garden, a mountain of presents..." continued Mom.

"And we bussed in hundreds of children from all over the state to pretend to be your friends," added Pop.

"Then you can do the same again today. And the next day. And the day after that. **WHERE ARE MY PANCAKES, BUTLER?!** And the day after that. And the day after that."

"And if we don't?" asked Mom.

Brad Junior thought for a moment. "If you don't, I will put you both in an old folks' home at the earliest opportunity and leave you there to **ROT!**"

Pop sighed. "I guess we'd better get going," he said.

"**YES!**" exclaimed Brad. "**PANCAKES! NOW!**"

Hopkins emerged from the kitchen carrying a silver platter.

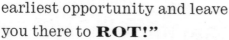

"Your pancakes, sir," the butler announced.

"That was too slow!" hissed Brad. "Pop, can you have him flogged?"

"No! That would be wrong, son."

"Shame," mused the boy.

Hopkins raised an eyebrow.

Hastily, preparations were made, and at four o'clock on the dot Brad's second birthday party in two days was in full swing. There was a huge disco tent on the lawn, a dolphin show in the swimming pool and a bouncy castle as big as the family mansion itself (though Brad decided as it was his birthday only he could bounce on it).

"Happy birthday!"

cried Mom and Pop as a giant chocolate cake was wheeled out.

"CAKE!" yelled the boy.
"Happy birthday to ME!"

With his hands, Brad scooped himself a humongous piece of cake and stuffed it in his mouth.

"Where are my presents?" he demanded, **spraying** crumbs all over the bussed-in guests, who looked a little bored as they had all been at his party yesterday.

Hopkins staggered along, holding a mountain of presents.

"Not enough!" said the boy. "Tomorrow I want more!"

The butler shook his head, and the presents tumbled to the ground. Mom and Pop looked at each other and sighed.

The next day it was the same story. Brad had yet another birthday party.

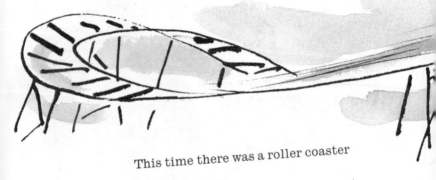

This time there was a roller coaster

on the lawn, an elephant to ride on and a famous pop star singing his hits on a little stage. Brad decided that

everyone else at the party had to wear headphones, so only he could hear the performance.

Once again, the biggest birthday cake anyone had ever seen was wheeled in by four servants.

"CAKE!" exclaimed the boy. "HAPPY BIRTHDAY TO ME!"

"What?" said Mom. She couldn't hear what her son had said because she still had her headphones on.

The boy shouted this time: "I SAID, 'HAPPY BIRTHDAY TO ME!' "

"Oh right! Yes! Happy birthday, Bradley Junior," said the lady.

Today the cake was the size of a paddling pool. With both hands, Brad scooped up as much of it as he possibly could and **stuffed** it in his face. The slice was, in fact, so big that what he left behind was smaller than what he took.

SPOILED BRAD

"WHERE ARE MY PRESENTS?!"
wailed the boy, spraying all his paid guests
from head to toe with crumbs.

"I WANT PRESENTS!"
Mom and Pop had learned their lesson yesterday.
Today there had to be more presents. So the butler
drove a forklift truck in, which was piled high with a
tower of gifts.

Brad took one look at what his parents had bought
him today and burst into tears.

"What's the matter now, Bradley Junior?" pleaded
Pop.

"I thought you loved me!" wailed the boy.
"And this is all you get me! Tomorrow I
want more. **Do you hear me?**
MORE!
MORE!
MORE!"

The next day at his birthday party he got more.
Much more. This time the garden played host
to a log flume, though Brad didn't go on it himself as
he **HATED** getting wet. There was a professional
heavyweight boxer, who Mom and Pop had paid to
pretend to be knocked out by their son with one punch.
There was a motorcycle display team, though the birthday
boy made all the other party guests wear blindfolds so
only he could see it. It was his birthday, after all. Of
course, it was his birthday every day now.

One of the children who'd been bussed in to
pretend to be one of Brad's friends made
the mistake of speaking up. "You
know, Brad, it's actually my
birthday today too."

The spoiled brat immediately started wailing.

"WHAA!"

"Whatever is the matter now?"
asked Pop.

"This spiteful little cockroach
has ruined my party!"

"How?" asked Pop.

"He said it's his birthday too."

"Well, it *is* my birthday!" replied the boy. "If I wasn't being paid a hundred dollars in cash to be here, I would be at home with my folks celebrating."

"I am not sharing my birthday party with anyone!" bawled Brad. "Please have him publicly horsewhipped."

"We can't have him horsewhipped, Brad!" replied Pop.

"Shame! Then have him thrown out immediately!" said Brad.

With that, two brutish security guards picked the boy up under his armpits and marched him out of the party.

"Will I still get my hundred bucks?" he asked as he was carried out.

"Right!" began Brad. "Because of that boy ruining my birthday, I want **double presents** today."

"Double presents is what we have," said Mom.
Right on cue, a huge crane swung overhead. At the
controls was the butler.

Swinging from the crane was a giant net, full
to bursting with presents. There must have
been thousands of them. There were so many they

blotted out the sun. Slowly the net of gifts was lowered to the ground.

"Are you happy now, Bradley Junior?" asked Pop.

"No, I am not!" replied the boy.

"Why not?"

"Because you've forgotten the cake! How can you have a birthday party with no cake?"

"We have got you a cake!" protested Mom.

The lady clicked her fingers and the biggest cake the world had ever seen was towed in by a tractor. This cake was the size of a swimming pool.

"CAKE!" shouted the boy. "Happy birthday to ME!"

As the paid guests joined in with a rather reluctant rendition of "Happy Birthday" – they had been singing for three days in a row now, after all – the boy clambered to the top of the pile of presents.

"What on earth are you doing, Bradley Junior?" called up Mom.

"I am going to dive into the cake!" replied the boy.

With that, the spoiled brat leaped up into the air and landed in the cake with a giant...

SPLOSH!

Cake flew over everybody and everything.

The boy started stuffing his face full of it. He was pushing more and more into his mouth as he tried to tread water* in the cake.

Eating huge amounts of chocolate cake every day had made the boy rather round, and soon Brad found himself sinking further and further into it. In moments he realised he was drowning in his own birthday cake.

"HELP ME!"

cried the boy.

Mom and Pop looked on, smiles creeping across their faces.

Hopkins spoke up. "Excuse me, sir, would you like me to dive in and rescue him?"

"Let's not be too hasty," replied Pop.

"Bradley Junior does love his cake," added Mom.

The butler smiled to himself.

* "Tread cake" is the correct expression here.

Slowly but surely, spoiled Brad sank lower and lower into the cake.

Soon he had disappeared from view, never to be seen again.

The lesson from this story is a simple one.

While you may be able to have your cake and eat it, don't be too greedy. **You might just drown in it.**

TRISH
the Troll

TOP

SECRET

SCRIBBLER

TRISH
the Troll

ONCE UPON A TIME, at the top of a very tall block of flats, lived a girl called Trish. From her window the little girl would look down upon the world, and daydream that she had complete power over everyone.

She would close one eye and hold her fingers up to the other. She would spot someone walking along fifty floors below – it might be an old lady walking her dog, a child playing with a ball or a young mother hurrying home with her shopping – and, whoever they were, Trish would get them in her sights and pretend she was squishing them between her fingers.

"You are squished, and you, and you…" she would say to herself, and a broad smile would spread across her face. "I will squish you all!"

Trish longed for some way of squishing people for real.

The idea came, as good ones often do, while she was sitting on the toilet. It was break-time at school, and Trish was sat on the loo, staring up at all the graffiti that decorated the walls and door. There was barely a space that wasn't covered by some words or drawings.

Some of the graffiti gave a newsflash on the love lives of the teachers:

MISS TROUT LOVES MR PRUFROCK.

I saw Mr Bongers and Miss Danube sitting in a tree K.I.S.S.I.N.G.!

MISS BIRCH HAS GOT THE HOTS FOR MR FUMBLE.

Other graffiti took the form of an alternative school report:

MATHS IS BORING!

I HATE HISTORY!

SCIENCE SUCKS!

There were quite a few harsh restaurant reviews of the school canteen:

DON'T EAT THE SAUSAGE ROLLS
UNLESS YOU WANT TO DIE!

YOU NEED TO CUT THE CUSTARD
WITH A KNIFE.

BRING BACK TURKEY TWIZZLERS!

Trish wondered what it would feel like if she wrote something really nasty. Would that be like squishing someone for real?

In her blazer pocket the girl kept a thick felt-tip pen. She placed the lid in her mouth as she pondered what to write. The most popular girl in school was Megan. Megan was always kind to the younger children, included all the other kids in games and had a smile for everyone, even the grumpiest teachers, like Mr Bongers. Finally Trish scribbled in big black letters:

MEGAN'S GOT BOG BREATH.

Megan didn't have bog breath. It didn't matter.

All that mattered to Trish was that once she had read it Megan would feel well and truly squished.

Trish left the cubicle, and walked past the mirror. As she glanced at herself, she noticed something startling. A big wart had appeared on the end of her nose.

"What is this?" muttered Trish to herself.

It was very strange. She hadn't noticed anything when she'd left her flat this morning. The girl pulled her hair down to hide it, and hurried off to her next lesson.

By lunchtime news had spread across the school like wildfire about what had been scrawled on the toilet wall. Poor Megan was crying and being comforted by her friends. Trish lingered nearby, munching on a Scotch egg so she could listen in.

"BOG BREATH?! I don't have bog breath, do I?" spluttered Megan through tears.

"NO!" came a chorus of girls' voices.

"Then why would anyone write such a thing?"

"I bet it's some saddo who gets a kick out of secretly being horrible," replied her best friend forever, Cheryl.

"I think they are called trolls," added a sporty boy called Paul, doing keepy-uppies.

"Who would want to upset you like that?" asked Trish with a guilty smirk. "You know I think you are the nicest girl in the whole school."

"Thanks so much," replied Megan. A gust of wind blew Trish's hair back, and Megan spotted the wart. It was so big it was hard to miss.

"Trish?" asked Megan.

"Yes?"

"What's that thingy?"

"What thingy?" asked Trish, playing innocent.

"That thingy on your nose," replied Megan.

"Oh, this tiny thingy? It's just a little zit. It will be gone in the morning."

But it hadn't gone in the morning. Trish woke up with a start, and immediately felt her nose.

"No!" she muttered to herself as she sat up in bed. "The wart is still there!"

No matter, there was more squishing to do.

The girl made sure she was first past the school gates that morning. The place was deserted, perfect for what Trish had planned. She sneaked into the Art room and snatched a pot of paint and a brush. From the shed she helped herself to the caretaker's ladder. Checking first that she was still alone, Trish daubed the outside of the main school building with letters so huge they could be read from outer space.

CHERYL HAS A MASSIVE BUM

As she slid down the ladder, the girl could feel her ears burning. She reached up to touch them.

"OUCH!"

They were flaming hot and growing at an alarming rate. **Thick** hairs started sprouting out of them.

PING!
PING!
PING!

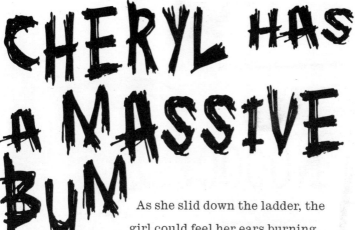

There was a puddle at her feet, so Trish peered at her reflection.

"Noooo!"

screamed the girl. She now had two ginormous furry ears that wouldn't have been out of place on a gorilla.

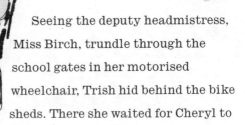

Seeing the deputy headmistress, Miss Birch, trundle through the school gates in her motorised wheelchair, Trish hid behind the bike sheds. There she waited for Cheryl to arrive. She couldn't wait to see her reaction...

The poor girl burst into floods of tears as soon as she saw the writing on the wall.

"I don't have a massive bum! Do I?" she wailed.

"No, your bottom is small," replied Megan.

"Too small?" demanded Cheryl.

"No!" said Paul. "Medium."

"Small medium or big medium?"

"Medium medium," replied the boy.

Trish sniggered to herself. Another victim squished.

BRIıNG!

The bell rang for the start of lessons. With her increasingly bizarre appearance, Trish wanted to wait until the coast was clear. As soon as the playground had emptied, the girl sneaked into the main school building. She paced along a deserted corridor on her way to her History lesson. Despite being late, she couldn't resist striking again. Trish pulled out her **thick** felt-tip pen and scrawled across the wall...

PAUL'S GOT A PIZZA FACE!

No sooner had she finished her poisonous prose than the girl noticed her hand had thick, curly hair growing on it.

"ARGH!"

she screamed. The girl checked her other hand. Before her very eyes her hands were becoming claws, her fingernails transforming into spiky talons.

"WHAT IS HAPPENING TO ME?!" she cried.

A classroom door swung open.

"Trish Tonking!" shouted Mr Bongers, the bald, bespectacled History teacher. "What's all this shouting?"

"Nothing, sir!"

"And you are late!"

"Sorry, sir!"

"Get in here at once!"

Trish took a deep breath, and walked towards her teacher. The girl pulled her hair down over her ears in the hope that she might hide them. Next she bowed her head and yanked down the sleeves of her blazer so Mr Bongers might not see her wart or claws.

She rushed past the teacher at the doorway, and hid at the back of the classroom.

"So where were we?" began Mr Bongers.

"The Vikings, sir," said Thomas, the cleverest boy in class.

"Oh yes, thank you, Thomas. The Vikings. Now, the Vikings had their own special beliefs. Can anyone tell me what they believed in?"

"Elves," replied Thomas confidently.

"Well done, Thomas," said the teacher. "That's right. *Elves* go up on the board. What else?"

The boy was first to put his hand up again.

"Anyone other than Thomas?" asked Mr Bongers. "Yes, Megan?"

"Giants?" guessed the girl.

"Excellent. *Giants* go up on the board. Any other thoughts? Anyone other than Thomas?"

As the children in the class continued making suggestions, Trish pulled a drawing pin off a poster on the wall and started *scratching* words on her desk. It was time to do more squishing. She smirked as she etched the words

THOMAS IS A THICKO

Just as she was rounding off the "O" of "THICKO", the girl felt a sharp pang of toothache.

"Aah!" It hurt.

Trish checked her reflection in the window. Her teeth were transforming into FANGS!

The girl looked so *terrifying* that she *terrified* herself. Her mouth widened in a silent scream.

"A TROLL!" shouted
Paul.

"Very good, Paul," said Mr
Bongers. "Put your hand up next
time, but you are correct. The
Vikings did indeed believe in trolls."

"No, sir! Look! A TROLL!"

exclaimed Paul, pointing frantically at Trish.

All eyes turned to the back of the class.

"ARGH!" screamed the other

children as Trish's blazer ripped...

RRRIIIPPP!!!

...and a thick back covered in
fur exploded out.

Next the girl's shoes
split open...

WwwRRRUUUPPP!!!

...and ten fat, dirty
toes broke out.

"BLEURGH!" Trish felt sick at the sight of them, the nails all black with goodness knows what.

Tentatively, Mr Bongers approached this thing that was sitting in his classroom.

"Are you feeling all right, Trish?" he asked. "It's just that you look like you have turned into some kind of, well… troll."

"I AM NOT A TROLL!" she growled. Trish's voice was suddenly **deeper and darker** than ever before. It was like listening to a hundred-year-old man who'd smoked a hundred cigarettes a day.

"Well, in fairness, Trish Tonking, you do look like a troll," replied the teacher.

"OH, BOG OFF, YOU BIG-NOSED BABOON!" she snarled.

Cheryl and Megan shared a look. The two girls had worked it out.

"TRISH MUST BE THE ONE WHO'S BEEN WRITING ALL THESE NASTY THINGS!" exclaimed Megan.

"SHUT YOUR FACE, THUNDER THIGHS!"

"SHE'S THE TROLL!" cried Cheryl.

Trish the troll had been busted.

She needed to get out of there. And fast. She dashed
to the door, but found she couldn't grip the handle with
her claws.

"STUPID DOOR!" she thundered, ramming
her shoulder up against it and smashing it off its
hinges. The door slammed to the floor.

B
A
N
G
!

B
O
O
M
!

"STOP THAT TROLL!" bellowed Mr Bongers.
As the creature scuttled down the corridor, all the
other classroom doors swung open, and teachers

and pupils swarmed out, eager to see who or what was causing the commotion. Soon there were hundreds of pupils and teachers giving chase. The one who looked most thrilled with it all was the ancient Miss Birch. The deputy head was in hot pursuit, going full speed ahead on her motorised wheelchair.

WHIRR! "FOLLOW ME, CHILDREN!" Miss Birch called out.

The troll turned a corner in the corridor only to see she was trapped. There were walls of people on either side of her.

"WATCH OUT! I WILL BITE!" shouted the creature, baring her fangs.

"Just you try," replied Miss Birch with a smile.

"CHARGE!" cried the old lady as she brandished her walking cane. Her wheelchair was trundling at full speed straight towards Trish.

In a desperate bid to escape, the troll leaped through the window... **SMASH!**

...before racing across the playground and out through the gates. Now the entire school was pursuing her. They were all shouting, and soon passers-by were joining in the chase.

"GET IT!" shouted the lollipop lady.
"CATCH IT!" yelled a traffic warden.
"LOCK IT UP!" called out a vicar.

Trish darted past her block of flats. People would know to find her there, so she dashed through some woods at the back of the flats. Soon she found herself in a spooky old churchyard. Exhausted, the troll lay down beside a gravestone.

"THIS WAY, EVERYONE!" called out Miss Birch, leading the pack in her motorised wheelchair. "I CAN SMELL IT!" The troll hid behind a tomb. The mob didn't spot her, and soon passed through the churchyard to continue their search for the creature.

Too full of fear to come out from her hiding place, the troll decided to stay put until nightfall. However, as soon as the sun went down the mob flooded

back into the churchyard, many brandishing flaming torches or pitchforks. "The footprints ended here," said Mr Bongers, now armed with a **huge** butterfly net.

"That means the creature must be hiding somewhere in the churchyard," replied Miss Birch, now armed with an antique musket.

The flaming torches were shone all around the graves. Before long, one stopped on a big hairy foot sticking out from behind a tomb.

"THERE IT IS!" shouted Mr Bongers.

"IT'S MINE!" called Miss Birch from her wheelchair as she raised her musket to take aim.

There was nothing else to do. Trish made a run for it.

BANG! BANG! Shots rang out.

Gunpowder lit up the sky.

The troll scrambled through a hedge, and tumbled down a steep bank before plunging into a freezing river below.

 PLOP!

The mob looked on from above as the flow of the water carried the creature off.

"BLAST!" cursed Miss Birch. "I am all out of gunpowder!"

After floating downriver all night, the troll found herself being swept out to sea.

"HELP!"

she screamed.

Soon the land was a distant memory.

Just as she thought the sea would take her, Trish spotted a tiny island. It was little more than a rock poking from the water. A wave **smashed** the troll into it. She clung on to the rock with her claws for dear life. With waves crashing around her, she just managed to heave herself up. The only shelter from the cruel sea was a cold, **dark** cave. Coughing and spluttering, Trish crawled into it.

That cave would become the troll's new home. It was so small she couldn't even stand up straight.

"Oh no!" cried Trish. "I am completely squished!"

Now she knew what it felt like. She passed the rest of her days all alone on that island.

Trish the troll lived unhappily ever after.

Competitive
COLIN

COLIN CLONT HATED BEING SHORT. He felt everyone was looking down on him the whole time. In fairness to them, they couldn't help it.

Every night Colin would lie in bed and curse his parents for being short and making him

short.

"It's not fair! Blast my titchy mum and dad. Because of them I will never be tall," he would say to himself. "But I will show everyone that I am a $giant$ among men!"

Colin had to win at **everything**. Rules and fair play meant nothing to him. He had to be the winner. *Number one.*

Because he was so competitive, Colin was not good company.

When playing Pass the Parcel at parties, he would **never, ever** let go of the parcel, even if the grown-up in charge spun it round the room to try to get him off it.

"I am **not** letting go!"

For Musical Chairs he was even worse. Colin would stick a chair to the bottom of his trousers with superglue at the start of the game so he couldn't lose.

"I am the winner!"

Once in a game of Hide-and-Seek
the boy hid in a chest of drawers for
a whole week because he was
so adamant he would never be
found, and that he'd be crowned
Hide-and-Seek Champion forever.

"Ha! Ha!"

Colin would watch TV quiz shows
and memorise the answers. Then
he would watch them on repeat
with his parents and **shout** out
all the answers before they could.

"I AM THE CLEVEREST!"

If the boy was taking part in a three-legged
race, he would borrow his grandma's
wooden leg and strap that to his own leg.
That way he wouldn't be slowed down
by being tied to anyone else.

"I won gold! Here's your leg back, Granny!" he
would shout as he hurled it across the playing field at her,
causing her to topple to the ground.

"OOF!"

COMPETITIVE COLIN

If Colin was losing badly at a board game, the boy would simply kick the board and all the counters up in the air, and pretend it was an accident as he crossed his legs.

BASH! "Let's just say I won that one."

In sack races Colin would cunningly conceal a mini-motorbike under his sack and *zoom* past the other children.

BRUMM!

When playing Musical Statues, Colin would dip himself in cement and let it dry first. That way he couldn't move a muscle and would win the game.

The downside was that he would have to be smashed out of the cement afterwards with a sledgehammer. **"Ouch!"**

In exams Colin would make sure he came top of
the class every time by using a mini-microphone, an
earpiece and a boy with a pile of textbooks outside, who
he had bribed with chocolate.

"A HUNDRED PER CENT AGAIN!"

In running races at school Colin would bring his own
starter pistol along. This he would only fire once he had
crossed the finish line.

"I won!" BANG!

In football matches Colin would tie the ball to
his boot so he never had to pass it, and it would be
impossible for anyone else other than him to score.

"GOAL!"

Most nights Colin would add a cup, medal or certificate to the huge trophy cabinet he had in his bedroom. Whenever he did win something, the boy gave himself a pat on the back.

"Well done, Colin," he would tell himself.

Because he had appeared to come top in everything, news soon spread. There were stories in local newspapers...

LOCAL LAD WINS A MEDAL OR SOMETHING DESPITE BEING SHORT

...before he broke through to national newspapers.

Eventually Colin found himself being interviewed on television.

WONDER KID! LITTLE BOY WINS BIG!

"That's a mightily impressive trophy cabinet, Colin," the presenter remarked.

"Thank you. I guess I am just the best at everything."

"And what's incredible is, looking at you, you can't be more than **five** years old."

"I am **ten**." "Oops."

Sitting in his oak-panelled office, watching the interview, was the head of the British Olympic team, Lord Sock. Sock was a portly old man with a bushy white moustache, who in the distant past had been an athlete himself.

"This boy is the answer to our prayers!" he exclaimed. "He is a winning machine."

The man looked up the boy's number and picked up the telephone right away.

RING RING! RING RING!

"Colin Clont?" he asked.

"Yes?"

"I am Lord Sock. You may have heard of me."

"Yes, of course, sir, I mean, lord."

"Our top athlete has just broken his leg in training, and it's the hundred-metre sprint on Saturday. Colin Clont, your country needs you to bring home the gold!"

The other end of the line went quiet. The boy felt sick to his stomach. Cheating in a school sports day was one thing, but **trickery** in the Olympic Games was quite another.

"Colin? Colin? Are you there?"

"Yes, I am here, Lord Sock."

The boy's mind was racing. He began to imagine the glory of winning. If he was the fastest man in the world, his height would never be mentioned again. A golden **haze** filled his head. There was no bigger competition in the world than the Olympic Games. There was no bigger prize than an **Olympic gold medal**. Competitive Colin couldn't help himself.

"Well, boy, have you made up your mind?"

"Yes, and it's a yes!"

"Splendid. We will see you at the British Olympic team training camp first thing tomorrow. It's only an hour away. Or for you, if you run, half an hour!"

"B-b-but, lord..." the boy spluttered. He looked at his trophy cabinet. He realised there wasn't one award he had received on merit. He had cheated **horrendously** to win everything.

"Yes, boy?"

"I prefer to train alone."

"Alone?" In all his years in sport, Lord Sock had never heard of such a thing.

"Yes. In my bedroom."

"Your bedroom?!" Now the man was utterly incredulous.

"Yes, lord."

"But this is the hundred-metre sprint! How big is your bedroom?"

"I don't know exactly, lord."

"Hazard a guess."

"Five metres across."

"Well, how are you going to practise running one hundred metres in such a small room?"

Colin thought for a moment. "I will run round in circles."

THE BOY HAD A POINT.

"Well, your sports record speaks for itself. We will see you on the day of the race. Don't let us down, Colin."

With that, Lord Sock hung up the telephone.

Colin felt **wobbly**, and slumped on to his bed. He was

going to have to think of something big if he was to pull off a victory at the Olympic Games.

That night he stayed awake until dawn dreaming up all the different ways he could cheat…

Fire himself out of a cannon and fly past the finish line.

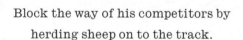

BOOM!

Block the way of his competitors by herding sheep on to the track.

"BAA!"

"BAA!"

Attach the back of the other competitors' underpants to **heavy weights** so as they set off they pinged straight back.

PING!

Tie everyone's shoelaces together so as soon as the starter pistol fires the runners all crash to the ground in a heap.

"Oof!"

Drive an ice-cream van on to the running track and serve all his fellow competitors free giant Mr Whippys, giving them indigestion before the race.

BURP!

Let off a **stink bomb** at the start line. **"POOH!"**

"Woof, Woof!"
Use a sleigh and a pack of huskies in the hope they might make him go faster.

Lie and tell everyone else it's actually an egg-and-spoon race, and distribute eggs and spoons to slow them all down.

CRACK!

Hitch a ride on the back of a cheetah, the world's fastest animal.

"Roar!"

Simply run faster than everyone else.

Sadly all these ideas seemed doomed to fail, especially the last one. Just as Colin was about to call the whole thing off, his imagination $swirl ed$ with the PERFECT PLAN.

Rocket-propelled shoes!

First, he bought the **biggest** running shoes he could find. These were at least twice the size of Colin's actual feet, and made him look like a clown.

Second, he hollowed out holes in the soles so he could install some wheels he had prised off his old toy cars.

Third, he laid his hands on the most **powerful** fireworks he could find. He cut open the backs of the shoes and placed the rockets inside.

While the other competitors would have to run as fast as they could, Colin would simply light the fuses on the fireworks and shoot past them in his special rocket-propelled shoes and win the gold medal.

What could possibly go wrong?

"Well, you are shorter than I expected," remarked
Lord Sock as he laid eyes on the boy for the first time.

"Oh, not you as well!" moaned Colin.

The pair were standing in the vast Olympic stadium
in Tokyo, Japan. The atmosphere was electric. Flags of
every country in the world flew. Hundreds of thousands
of sports fans were packed in their seats. Cameras from
around the globe were beaming every event live to an
audience of **BILLIONS**.

The man looked down at the boy's enormous running shoes. "My, what huge feet you have."

Colin's shoes were nearly as long as he was tall. He'd been hoping no one would notice how big they were, but it was impossible not to.

"Thank you, lord. That's why I can run so fast."

"Is it really, boy?"

"Well, I say 'run'… I do have an unusual way of running, where my feet never leave the ground."

Lord Sock could not hide his shock. "I am extremely concerned about this, boy. You are representing our great country (and it is a great country as it has 'great' in its title) in the most important sporting event in the world. And you tell me you run without your feet ever leaving the ground? I have never heard so much nonsense in all my life. Colin, I am pulling you from the race."

"No, lord. Please. I will win gold. **I PROMISE YOU.**"

A towering figure passed the boy. This was Ike Scarper, representing Jamaica. He was the fastest man in the world, with 103 Olympic gold medals to his name. He looked at Colin and chuckled to himself.

"Ha! Ha! Ha!" Ike headed straight for the racetrack.

"You'd better get going, boy," said Lord Sock.

With some difficulty, Colin rolled to the start line.

An Olympic official dressed in a blazer stepped up to the track, starting pistol in hand.

"Take your places at the start line, gentlemen."

Ike was next to Colin. When the man crouched, he was still taller than Colin when he was standing up.

"How nice for the clown to lend you his shoes!" murmured Ike with a smirk.

Colin shook his head.

He was desperate to teach this handsome, funny and – worst of all – tall man a lesson. The boy reached into his shorts and pulled out a craftily concealed box of matches.

"On your marks!" called out the official.

"I'll be waiting at the finish line with a cup of British tea for you!" said Ike.

Colin lit the fuse in his left shoe.

"Get set!"

However, Colin's fingers burned, and he dro$_{pp_{ed}}$ the match before he could light the next fuse.

"Ow!"

This could spell disaster. BANG!

The starter pistol fired.

The athletes powered towards the finish line led, as always, by Ike Scarper.

With only one firework lit and his right foot being dragged along behind, Colin found it impossible to go in a straight line. Instead, he shot off sideways and smashed into one of the runners.

THUMP!

"OOF!"

"ARGH!"

Colin sent the man flying.

The runner fell to the ground. THUD!

Spinning around uncontrollably like a giraffe

at its first roller disco, Colin took out a few

more runners.

THUMP!
THUMP!
THUMP!
"OOF!"
"OOF!"
"OOF!"

They fell to the ground.
THUD! THUD!
THUD!

Now *spinning* on one leg like an

ice-dance routine gone horribly wrong,

Colin's other foot with its giant shoe

spun around, clumping

some of the other runners in the face.

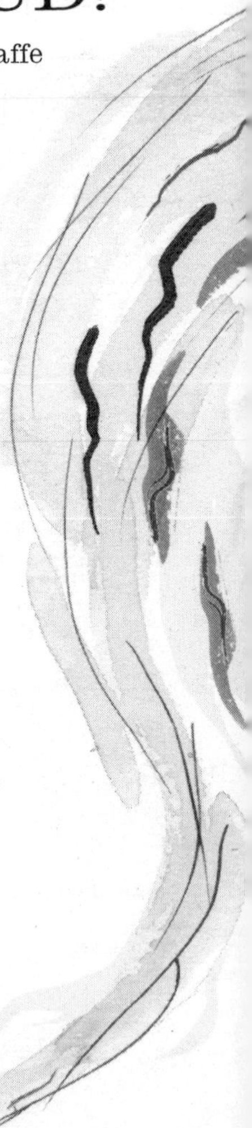

"OW!"
"OW!"
"OW!"

They fell to the ground in a heap.

T
H
U
M
P!

Soon there was just one man standing. It was, of course, the Olympic legend **Ike Scarper**. Just as he was about to cross the finish line and win his 104th Olympic gold medal, the firework in Colin's shoe

exploded...

BANG!

...sending the boy flying up towards the sky.

W
H
O
O
S
H!

Colin's huge rocket-propelled shoe zoomed through the air, his little body flailing behind. He shot high above the clouds. The boy rather liked it up there. It was calm and peaceful. For a moment Colin was suspended there, perfectly still. But what goes up must come down. At speed. Looking far below he could see Ike Scarper was about to cross the finish line, but when he looked up Colin landed on top of him...

"OW!"

...knocking him out **COLD**.

Ike Scarper fell to the ground like a mighty oak.

THUD!

Sitting on top of the man, all the boy had to do now was stand up and cross over the finish line. He held up his hands in triumph.

The crowd in Tokyo was furious.

"BOO!"

This little British boy had wrecked the race, and knocked out the world's fastest man.

"That was a disgrace!" thundered Lord Sock as he marched up to the boy. "You should be ashamed of yourself. You have let the Olympics down. You have let Great Britain down. Most of all, you have let yourself down."

Before Colin could reply, a voice boomed over the loudspeaker system. "The winner of the hundred-metre sprint is Colin Clont of Great Britain!"

The boos became louder still.

"BOO!"

Before he knew it, the Olympic officials had whisked Colin off to the winners' podium. There he was not only

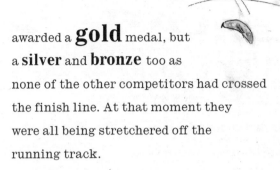

awarded a **gold** medal, but
a **silver** and **bronze** too as
none of the other competitors had crossed
the finish line. At that moment they
were all being stretchered off the
running track.

Colin's smug face was beamed around
the world as a hundred thousand
people in the stadium and billions
around the world b o o e d him.

"BOOOO!"

From that moment, Colin Clont became public enemy
number one. The boy couldn't walk down the street
anywhere in the world without strangers booing him,
and even throwing rotten fruit at him.

SPLAT!

"BOO!" THWACK! "CHEAT!"
"OOF!"
"HISS!" SPLUT!

This meant Colin could never go out. He had to stay in his bedroom with the curtains closed in case some angry passer-by hurled a rotten tomato at the window.

SPLURGE!

The boy's three Olympic medals took pride of place in his trophy cabinet. Every night before he went to bed he placed them round his neck, and admired himself in the mirror.

"I am the only person to have ever come first, second and third in the same race," he would tell himself. "That means I am the absolute BEST and not short at all."

Then the boy would give himself a little pat on the back, and sit alone in his

DARKENED ROOM.

No No
NOE

ONCE THERE LIVED a little girl called Noe. Noe only ever used one word, and that word was "no". It was a word she loved. It was a word that if you said it enough would drive everyone else crazy.

Nothing gave Noe greater pleasure than seeing the chaos the word "no" caused. She thought of the word as a stick of dynamite. If you used enough of them, you could cause a huge EXPLOSION.

KABOOM!

Whatever her mum or dad asked her to do at home, the answer was always the same.

"Noe, please can you clean your room now?"

"No!"

"Noe, don't be greedy! Please can you leave one of those chocolates for me?"

"No!"

"NOE! WILL YOU TURN YOUR MUSIC DOWN?!"

"No!"

Soon her mum and dad would be hopping up and down on the spot with fury.

"NO, NO, NOE!"

At school Noe found the word "no" had an even more maddening effect.

Our story begins one morning in the school playground when Noe was slurping a thick chocolate milkshake.

When the girl had had enough, she threw the half-full paper cup at the headmaster's feet, splattering his shoes and trousers with chocolate milkshake. As always, Mr Gubbins was dressed immaculately in a three-piece suit with a natty bow tie. He HATED litter, and wanted the whole school to be spotless like him.

"Noe? Pick up your litter at once!" demanded the headmaster.

"No."

"YES!"

"No."

"You will pick up your litter at once!"

"No."

Mr Gubbins was turning scarlet with fury.

"Noe! See me in my office at once!"

"No."

"Right, you have a detention!"

"No."

"A double detention!"

"No!"

"Well, I... er, I um, I am excluding you from school with immediate effect!"

"No!"

"Right, that's it! That's my last warning. Do you understand me?"

The veins in Mr Gubbins's head were throbbing now.

"No," replied the little girl with a smirk. Noe rarely got such a huge reaction from her favourite little word.

"I mean that I am not giving you any more warnings.
I think you already knew that, didn't you, Noe?"

"No."

"Well, I think you do, Noe."

"No."

"Yes."

"No."

"Yes."

"No."

The headmaster then tried to
trick Noe, by saying "no"
instead of "yes".

"No."

Noe paused for a moment
before saying, **"No.**"

Gubbins dropped
to his hands and
knees, and began howling
like a wolf.

"A-WOOOOOOOOOOO!"

It was clear the man couldn't take a moment more of this. Soon all the pupils in the school had gathered around. They were interested to see if their headmaster might actually burst like a balloon.

Fortunately the old caretaker, Mr Potts, was at the other side of the playground pulling some leaves out of his beard. Seeing the commotion, the old man hobbled over. He took his boss by the arm and laid him down on a comfy bed of leaves in his wheelbarrow.

"Come along now, Mr Gubbins, sir," he whispered.

As he wheeled the headmaster away, Potts shot a disapproving look at Noe, who just smirked back.

The episode got Potts pondering... If only he could find some way to get the girl to finally say "yes", then the world would be a better place.

The problem was that "yes" was a word Noe never, ever said. To her, "yes" was a boring word. It didn't drive people crazy.

Over the years Noe had become famous at her school for driving all her teachers round the bend.

Mr Nimbus the Geography teacher had become so frustrated at Noe saying "no" to everything on a trip to the countryside that he went missing. He wasn't found for six months. When he was finally unearthed, he was living on a diet of rainwater and soil in a cave in just his underpants.

Noe's PE teacher, Miss Spriggot, became so exasperated that Noe refused to do any exercise of any kind ever that she burst into tears, and went and locked herself in the toilet. The teacher didn't come out for a whole term. She survived by having biscuits passed under the gap in the door. Tea was poured under too that she had to lap up with her tongue like a dog.

NO NO NOE

The head of Drama at the school fared little better. When the class was practising improvisation or "improv", as Mr Snood called it, all Noe would say was **"no"**. The first rule of "improv" was always say **"yes"**. After years of this Mr Snood couldn't take any more and was found in the school canteen repeatedly hitting himself over the head with a wooden spoon.

When Noe said **"no"** to doing anything the teacher asked in Science lessons, poor Mrs Ledement ate her own shoes. She said later that it was a cry for help.

The most serious incident of all involved the Art teacher, Miss Knicknocks. When all Noe would paint on the canvas was the word **"NO"** again and again and again, Miss Knicknocks dipped her bottom in blue paint and ran around the school pressing her behind against every surface she could see. There were bottom prints on every wall, door and window. She is now on PERMANENT "gardening leave".

As for Noe, she delighted in all the chaos she caused. The girl was determined to say **"no"** to absolutely everything for the rest of her life.

One day Potts was in the local newsagent's buying some of his beloved toffee bonbons. On Friday afternoons after finishing work he would buy himself a bag that he would enjoy over the weekend.

"There you are, Mr Potty! A bag of my *finest bonbons*," said the newsagent as he poured them into a brown paper bag. "To you, sir, my favourite customer, the bag is absolutely **FREE OF CHARGE**."

"Thank you, Raj," said the caretaker.

"But please bring the bag back. It's the only one I have."

D
I
N
G!

The bell on the door rang as Noe stepped into the shop.

Raj grimaced as he saw her.

"Ah, Miss Noe who always says 'no'! My fav—" Raj couldn't bring himself to say it. "One of my top five hundred customers."

It was clear that the newsagent didn't look forward to Noe's visits to his shop. Potts was intrigued how someone who only ever said "no" would be able to order some sweets, so he lingered over by the magazine rack, pretending to browse.

"Can I help you at all, Miss Noe-No?" asked Raj.

"No," replied the girl.

The newsagent sighed to himself. "This is always a trial. Miss Noe-No, would you like your usual bag of liquorice allsorts?"

The girl hesitated. Noe badly wanted those liquorice allsorts. In fact, her mouth was watering as her eyes fixed on the jar behind Raj's head.

The newsagent tried again. "Miss Noe-No, do you NOT want a bag of liquorice allsorts?"

"No."

"So that means you **do**!" exclaimed Raj. "Is **that** right, Miss Noe-No?"

"No!" The girl couldn't help herself. She stamped her foot on the floor. It was clear that saying "no" all the time drove Noe nuts too. Mr Potts was still pretending to browse through a copy of *Woman's Weekly* as he munched on his toffee bonbons, intrigued by what he saw.

"Oh my," exclaimed Raj. "This is going to take all night again! Can you just for once in your life say 'yes', please, Miss Noe-No?!"

"NO!"

"All right, young Miss Noe-No!" Raj was getting annoyed now. "See how you like this! Do you **not** not **not** not **not** want a bag of liquorice allsorts?"

A look of deep confusion crossed the girl's normally smug-looking face. There were just too many "not"s for her to count.

"Or do you **not** **not** not not **not** not **not** not **not** want a bag?"

The girl was looking increasingly frustrated.

"Or perhaps you do not **not** **not** not **not** not **not** not **not** not not **not** not **not** infinity and no returns want a bag of liquorice allsorts?"

Noe growled at Raj, and then ran out of the shop, knocking over a display of out-of-date Easter eggs.

"I got you, Miss Noe-No!"

D
I
N
G
!

"Ha! Ha!"

Raj chuckled to himself.

"That was very clever, Raj!" mumbled Mr Potts, still chewing on a toffee bonbon.

"Thank you, Mr Pottiness! That's the way to trick that annoying little miss! Put so many 'not's in front of her that she can't possibly count them."

"I will be sure to tell the teachers at school. She drives them all up the wall."

"You do that, sir. Now, could I have my bag back, please?"

The caretaker looked down into his bag of bonbons. "Raj, I've still got a dozen left."

"Well, pop them all in your mouth, chop-chop!"

"I like the bag to last me the weekend!"

"Chew them very slowly then!"

Reluctantly Potts poured the rest of the bonbons into his mouth. It was so **full** his cheeks looked like two balloons.

"Thank you so much, Mr Pottery," said Raj as he took back the brown paper bag and folded it up neatly. "See you next Friday!" D I N G!

The caretaker had all weekend to work on his plan. As soon as he had managed to gulp down the huge mouthful of bonbons, he called the headmaster and told him of the scheme.

"But, sir, this will only work if every single teacher, dinner lady, secretary, cleaner and, of course, every single one of the pupils takes part."

"I understand. And, Mr Potts? Why don't you change all the signs in the school over the weekend? Fingers crossed that will really annoy Noe!"

"You will teach that girl a lesson."

"We all will!"

As soon as Potts had put the telephone down, he set to work.

All the signs up and down the school were to be changed.

"DO NOT RUN IN THE CORRIDOR" became

DO NOT not **not** not not not NOT **not** NOT not **not** RUN IN **THE CORRIDOR.**

"DO NOT PLAY BALL GAMES HERE" became

DO NOT NOT **NOT** NOT NOT **NOT** NOT **NOT** NOT NOT **NOT**
NOT NOT NOT **NOT** NOT **NOT** NOT NOT
NOT PLAY BALL GAMES HERE.

And "DO NOT TALK IN THE LIBRARY" became

DO NOT NOT NOT NOT NOT NOT NOT
NOT NOT NOT NOT NOT **NOT** NOT NOT **NOT** NOT
NOT NOT **NOT** NOT NOT NOT **NOT** NOT **NOT**
NOT NOT NOT TALK IN THE LIBRARY.

Monday morning couldn't come soon enough for
Mr Gubbins. The headmaster was buzzing with
excitement. As Noe was always late for school
(normally delaying a bus full of people by saying "no"
to paying her fare), Mr Gubbins called an assembly for
the entire school.

"Today we are all going to play a trick
on Noe, the girl who just says 'no'."

"HOORAY!" Everyone erupted
in cheers.

Miss Knicknocks, who had ended up putting blue bottom prints everywhere, had been called back into school by the headmaster. The Art teacher did not want to miss this.

"Every time you ask Noe a question, put as many 'not's into it as possible. That way she will become confused, and not not not not not not not know whether to say 'no' or not."

The crowd listened intently.

"If anyone gets Noe to say 'yes', then we won't have any more lessons today!" announced the headmaster.

Another huge cheer went up.

"WHOO!"

"In fact, we will have a

HUGE PARTY!"
"WHOOOOOOOO!"

The caretaker was standing on a stepladder in the assembly hall, peering out of the window, keeping watch for Noe's arrival.

"She's coming!" Mr Potts called out as he saw the girl pass through the school gates.

"Right!" said the headmaster. "Everyone act natural!"

When you are told to act naturally, it can immediately seem impossible to do. Carrying a secret around feels like holding a huge wobbly jelly. You feel as if you are going to drop it at any moment.

All the children swarmed into the playground, and bombarded Noe with questions.

"Noe, do you not **not** not not **not** not not not not want to come to my house for tea?"

"Noe, do you not not not not not not not not not **not** not not not want one of my crisps?"

"Noe, do you not not **not** not not not not not not not not not not not not not **not** not want to copy my Maths homework?"

"Noe, do you **not** not not not not **not** not not not not not not not **not** not not not not not want to go on a date with Ned Shabby?"

The girl became so frustrated she felt as if her head was going to explode. How had she become trapped in this nightmare where she couldn't say no?

The girl dashed into the school building and hurried along the corridor. She put her hands over her ears as more and more of these unanswerable questions were fired at her like a machine gun.

RAT- TAT-TAT!

Having drowned out everyone's voices, Noe suddenly spotted the sign on the wall that read...

DO NOT NOT NOT NOT NOT NOT NOT NOT NOT NOT RUN IN THE CORRIDOR.

What on earth was going on?!

"ARGH!" Noe screamed again.

The girl stopped dead in the corridor, not knowing which way to turn.

"Noe, do you not **not** not not not not not **not** not not not not not not not **not** not not not not not not **not** not **not** not not not not not not not not not not not not not not not not **not** not not not **not** not not not not not not not not **not** not not **not** not not not want to bunk off later?" piped up another child.

"Noe, do you **not** not not not not not not **not** not not **not** not not not not not **not** not **not** not not not not not not not not not not not not not **not** not not not not not not not not **not** not not **not** not not **not** not not **not** not not not want to sign up for the school trip to the zoo?" said another.

"Noe, do you **not** not not not not not not **not** not not **not** not not not not not **not** not not not not not not **not** not not not not **not** not not not not not **not** not not not not not not not not not **not** not not not not **not** not not not not not **not** not not **not** not not not not not not not not **not** not not not want me to give you my dinner money?" asked a third.

"AAARRRGG GHHH!" screamed Noe.

The girl made a dash for it, and ran into her English classroom. She slammed the door behind her. **BAM!**

Then she breathed a sigh of relief. However, when she turned round, Noe realised all her teachers were there, staring back at her.

"Hello, Noe," said Mr Nimbus the Geography teacher brightly. "Do you **not** not not not not not **not** not not **not** not not not not not **not** not not not not not **not** not not not **not** not not not **not** not not not not **not** not not not **not** not not not **not** not not **not** not not not **not** not not **not** not **not** not not not **not** not **not** not not **not** not not **not** not not **not** not not **not** not not **not** not not **not** not not **not** not not **not** not not not **not** not **not** not **not** not not **not** not not **not** not **not** not **not** not not **not** not **not** not **not** not not not not not **not** want to do your homework?"

"ARGH!"

Noe felt as if she was going bananas.

The tracksuited PE teacher Miss Spriggot's turn was next. "Noe, do you **not** not not **not** not not not **not** not not not not not not **not** **not** not not not **not** not not **not** not **not** not not **not** not **not** not not **not** not not not **not** not not not **not** not not **not** not **not** not not **not** not **not** not **not** not not **not** not not **not** not not not not **not** not **not** not **not** not **not** not **not** not **not** not **not** not **not** not **not** not not **not** not not not **not** not not not not **not** not not not **not** not not want to do the cross-country run this year?"

"AARRGGHH!'

Noe was becoming so irritated her face had turned the colour of beetroot and her hair was standing up on end.

Last it was Mr Snood's turn. "Noe, do you think that drama is **not** not no**t** **not** no**t** not not no**t** **NOT** not no**t** not no**t** no**t** **NOT** not not not **not** not no**t** **not** not **not** not not **not** not not **not** not no**t** **not** not no**t** **not** not no**t** **NOT** not not **not** not not **not** not no**t** **NOT** not not **not** no**t** **NOT** not **NOT** not **not** **NOT** not **not** not **NOT** not **not** not no**t** **not** not not **not** not no**t** **not** not no**t** not **not** not no**t** **not** not not not **not** not not not **not** not not **not** not **NOT** not not no**t** not not **NOT** not not a stupid subject or **not** not no**t** **not** no**t** not not **NOT** not not not no**t** not **NOT** **not** not not **not** not no**t** **not** not **NOT** not no**t** not not **not** not no**t** **not** not no**t** **not** not no**t** **not** not not **not** not no**t** not not **not** not no**t** **not** not **NOT** not not **not** not **NOT** not **NOT** not no**t** **NOT** not **not** not **NOT** not **not** not no**t** **not** not no**t** **not** **not** not not not not not not no**t** not?"

"AAARRRGG GHHH!" _{screamed Noe.}

The girl couldn't take it any more.

Then the headmaster appeared in the doorway. "Noe, would you like us to stop asking you these stupid questions?"

All the staff looked at the girl with anticipation, as did Mr Potts the caretaker and the children who had gathered outside the windows of the classroom.

"YES!" she finally cried.

The entire school erupted into cheers. **"HOORAY!"**

"HA HA!" cried Mr Gubbins.

"WE DID IT!" exclaimed Mrs Ledement the Science teacher, who had previously been reduced to eating her own shoes. She grabbed Mr Snood and planted a lingering kiss on his bald head, which he did not seem to like at all.

"EURGH!" uttered the Drama teacher.

Mr Potts rushed into the classroom, and the headmaster held out his arms to embrace him.

"You are a genius, Mr Potts!"

"Oh, it wasn't my idea. It was Raj the newsagent!"

"Well, that's splendid as I have asked him to help with the party in the playground. Let's all head out and see what he has in store for us."

Once the teachers had rushed past him, the headmaster was left alone with Noe.

"Noe, are you pleased that we finally got you to say

'yes'?" asked the man as he straightened his bow tie.

The girl thought for a moment. It felt as if a great weight had been lifted from her. She smiled and said, "No!"

"What?!"

"I am only joking, sir. Yes! YES! YES! I am pleased. I love the word 'YES'!"

"YES, YES, YES!" exclaimed Mr Gubbins.

The headmaster led the way out to the party in the playground.

There was a mobile disco, and the teachers were all boogieing on down as the pupils sniggered at them. The always-generous Raj had set up a stall of free sweets.

"Come and get your sweeties here!" called the newsagent.

On the far side of the playground Mr Potts had set up a **HUGE** firework display. The caretaker lit the fuse, and then in an explosion of sparkles a word was spelled out in giant letters...

Noe looked at the display, and turned to Mr Potts. She said, "What a *beautiful* word it is."